G R JORDAN

Save The King

A Highlands and Islands Detective Thriller #45

First published by Carpetless Publishing 2025

Copyright © 2025 by G R Jordan

All rights reserved. No part of this publication may be reproduced, stored or transmitted in any form or by any means, electronic, mechanical, photocopying, recording, scanning, or otherwise without written permission from the publisher. It is illegal to copy this book, post it to a website, or distribute it by any other means without permission.

This novel is entirely a work of fiction. The names, characters and incidents portrayed in it are the work of the author's imagination. Any resemblance to actual persons, living or dead, events or localities is entirely coincidental.

G R Jordan asserts the moral right to be identified as the author of this work.

G R Jordan has no responsibility for the persistence or accuracy of URLs for external or third-party Internet Websites referred to in this publication and does not guarantee that any content on such Websites is, or will remain, accurate or appropriate.

Designations used by companies to distinguish their products are often claimed as trademarks. All brand names and product names used in this book and on its cover are trade names, service marks, trademarks and registered trademarks of their respective owners. The publishers and the book are not associated with any product or vendor mentioned in this book. None of the companies referenced within the book have endorsed the book.

For avoidance of doubt, no part of this publication may be used in any manner for purposes of training artificial intelligence technologies to generate text, including without limitation, technologies that are capable of generating works in the same style or genre as the Work.

First edition

ISBN (print): 978-1-917497-25-1
ISBN (digital): 978-1-917497-24-4

This book was professionally typeset on Reedsy.
Find out more at reedsy.com

The king must die so that the country can live.

                Maximilien Robespierre

Contents

Foreword	iii
Acknowledgments	iv
Books by G R Jordan	v
Chapter 01	1
Chapter 02	10
Chapter 03	18
Chapter 04	26
Chapter 05	35
Chapter 06	44
Chapter 07	53
Chapter 08	62
Chapter 09	71
Chapter 10	79
Chapter 11	88
Chapter 12	97
Chapter 13	105
Chapter 14	114
Chapter 15	122
Chapter 16	130
Chapter 17	138
Chapter 18	147
Chapter 19	155
Chapter 20	163
Chapter 21	172

Chapter 22	182
Chapter 23	190
Chapter 24	198
Chapter 25	206
Read on to discover the Patrick Smythe series!	212
About the Author	215
Also by G R Jordan	217

Foreword

The events of this book, while based around real and also fictitious locations around the UK, are entirely fictional and all characters do not represent any living or deceased person. All companies are fictitious representations and locations have been modified for the purposes of the story. This novel is best read while wearing a large crown—but keep your head down!

Acknowledgments

To Ken, Jean, Colin, Evelyn, John and Rosemary for your work in bringing this novel to completion, your time and effort is deeply appreciated.

Books by G R Jordan

The Highlands and Islands Detective series (Crime)

1. Water's Edge
2. The Bothy
3. The Horror Weekend
4. The Small Ferry
5. Dead at Third Man
6. The Pirate Club
7. A Personal Agenda
8. A Just Punishment
9. The Numerous Deaths of Santa Claus
10. Our Gated Community
11. The Satchel
12. Culhwch Alpha
13. Fair Market Value
14. The Coach Bomber
15. The Culling at Singing Sands
16. Where Justice Fails
17. The Cortado Club
18. Cleared to Die
19. Man Overboard!
20. Antisocial Behaviour
21. Rogues' Gallery
22. The Death of Macleod - Inferno Book 1

23. A Common Man - Inferno Book 2
24. A Sweeping Darkness - Inferno Book 3
25. Dormie 5
26. The First Minister - Past Mistakes Book 1
27. The Guilty Parties - Past Mistakes Book 2
28. Vengeance is Mine - Past Mistakes Book 3
29. Winter Slay Bells
30. Macleod's Cruise
31. Scrambled Eggs
32. The Esoteric Tear
33. A Rock 'n' Roll Murder
34. The Slaughterhouse
35. Boomtown
36. The Absent Sculptor
37. A Trip to Rome
38. A Time to Rest
39. Cinderella's Carriage
40. Wild Swimming
41. The Wrong Man
42. Drop Like Flies
43. Someone Else's Ritual
44. None Too Precious
45. Save the King
46. The Silent War

Kirsten Stewart Thrillers (Thriller)

1. A Shot at Democracy
2. The Hunted Child
3. The Express Wishes of Mr MacIver
4. The Nationalist Express
5. The Hunt for 'Red Anna'
6. The Execution of Celebrity
7. The Man Everyone Wanted
8. Busman's Holiday
9. A Personal Favour
10. Infiltrator
11. Implosion
12. Traitor

Jac Moonshine Thrillers

1. Jac's Revenge
2. Jac for the People
3. Jac the Pariah

Siobhan Duffy Mysteries

1. A Giant Killing
2. Death of the Witch
3. The Bloodied Hands
4. A Hermit's Death

The Contessa Munroe Mysteries (Cozy Mystery)

1. Corpse Reviver
2. Frostbite
3. Cobra's Fang

The Patrick Smythe Series (Crime)

1. The Disappearance of Russell Hadleigh
2. The Graves of Calgary Bay
3. The Fairy Pools Gathering

Austerley & Kirkgordon Series (Fantasy)

1. Crescendo!
2. The Darkness at Dillingham
3. Dagon's Revenge
4. Ship of Doom

Supernatural and Elder Threat Assessment Agency (SETAA) Series (Fantasy)

1. Scarlett O'Meara: Beastmaster

Island Adventures Series (Cosy Fantasy Adventure)

1. Surface Tensions

Dark Wen Series (Horror Fantasy)

1. The Blasphemous Welcome
2. The Demon's Chalice

Chapter 01

Detective Chief Inspector Seoras Macleod heard the door of his office open after an abrupt knock. The person outside had waited for the customary 'Come in' but then had approached anyway, despite Seoras not having said. She was getting to know him, clearly.

Currently, Macleod was deep in thought, looking out of the window. He hadn't gone home, his mind musing on the tactical plan he was putting into place. He had to get them. This had to be closed down. Last time had been too close. His team were hunting for the Forseti group, people above the law, enforcing their own justice.

Forseti, a Norse god Macleod had never heard of, had seemed to inspire them. So much so that they were buried in the idea of sacrificial knives and a world that wasn't based on law and order, at least not his version of it. People who tried to control society, and they'd brought out the beast from those in the criminal classes.

Not that they'd just attacked the criminal classes. Innocents had been killed along the way, and it all started with Gavin Isbister, Macleod's former partner, albeit a short-lived connection. Still, Isabel, Gavin Isbister's wife, was safe now. Macleod had got her away from a lifetime of having to be married to someone she didn't care about. Someone who was watching her, controlling her, making sure that the truth about what had happened to Gavin didn't come out.

It wasn't the ideal time either, Macleod had thought. His thoughts were on Hope McGrath, thinking back to when he'd first met her. They'd gone to Lewis together to solve the case of a poor girl who'd been knifed. Macleod hadn't known McGrath well back then. He'd seen her as brazen—a hussy as his mum might have called her, and yet she was nothing of the sort. Now she was expecting, and the one thing he didn't want was her here, involved in this. Yes, she said she would stay in the office behind a desk, but this was Hope—could she really keep to that?

And then he thought of Clarissa. She'd gone over to Heligoland, albeit with Kirsten—his former colleague, and now a freelance spy, if that was the correct terminology. He'd sent Kirsten with her, thank goodness. Clarissa, for all that she could bulldoze her way in, for all that she earned the name 'the Rottweiler,' she'd been out of her depth—just like he had in Italy. And then there was Emmett, someone he was still trying to understand.

'I take it you wanted this coffee?' said a voice behind him.

He turned and smiled. Tanya gave him a soft beam, and then, with eyes that were sympathetic, poured him his coffee.

'You don't have to do that, you know. I can do all this.'

'I'm your personal assistant, and I can tell when you're in deep. I am right? Could tell when I knocked; there was nothing, no response. Did you even hear me?'

'Oh, I hear it,' said Macleod. 'It's just that—'

'You don't have to tell me,' said Tanya. 'I know things have

CHAPTER 01

been a bit, well . . .'

'Yes, they have,' said Macleod, 'but that will change. Have you been watching? Have you been taking care of yourself?'

'I read the instructions Miss Stewart gave us. Is it really that bad?'

'Certain people think it could be,' said Macleod. He was referring to the fact that the team was now under pressure from both sides of the current investigation. The Forseti group and those from what he termed as the Revenge group—the criminals who had been attacked by the Forseti group—were coming after the team. There was no safe place anymore. And as such, Macleod had asked Kirsten to assist those who needed to keep a better eye out for themselves than they normally would.

He'd understood the necessity of this from his time in Italy, when Kirsten had saved his life. This was unfamiliar territory, not policing as he knew it. The Assistant Chief Constable had decided that Macleod should go out on his own, run a team with all his people, and bring down both sides of the equation. Today was day one, and they were about to meet all together for the first time. But they were to meet in Hope's office. Macleod didn't want it brought up to any conference room where they would be seen, didn't want it out among the corridors of the station where people would wonder what they were doing. The idea of his people meeting downstairs in Hope's office wasn't a strange one.

Macleod's phone rang and Tanya picked it up. 'Detective Chief Inspector Macleod's office. How can I help?'

Macleod saw that Tanya nearly burst out laughing, but she straightened her face before putting the phone down.

'Who was that?' asked Macleod.

'Apparently,' said Tanya, 'a DI Urquhart is eager for your presence.'

'And she said that?'

'Well, she phrased it differently.'

'Differently?'

'Well, you might say badly.'

'How badly can you phrase "Is he ready?"'

Tanya looked away for a moment.

'I won't tell her,' said Macleod.

'"Tell him to get his arse down here,"' said Tanya.

Macleod grinned. 'I'll take this coffee to go then,' he said.

'Do you need me there?' asked Tanya.

'No,' said Macleod. 'I don't want to give you too many details. You helped us already, and it was much appreciated, but the less you know, the less you could give out.'

'It's okay,' said Tanya. 'You wouldn't have got Miss Stewart to give me those instructions if you didn't think it was serious. I understand.'

Macleod lifted the coffee cup up to his lips and sipped.

'When Perry recommended you,' said Macleod, 'he didn't mention this.'

'Didn't mention what?'

'You really know how to make coffee, don't you?'

He watched Tanya smile as he left his office, cup held before him, one hand in front of it. Trying to make sure he didn't spill it, Macleod made his way down the stairs, round, and into the offices of Hope McGrath's team. Her office lay off to the side, and the main office was devoid of anyone. As he looked into Hope's personal office, he saw why. They were all there, except for the injured Perry. The door was open for him, and a chair was available beside the round table he used to call his own.

A screen was illuminated behind the table around which Hope, Clarissa, and Emmett waited. The rest of the team were all perched on the edges of desks, or up against the wall. Macleod saw that Perry, not due to be discharged from the hospital until later that day, was not the only one missing. Clarissa's new team—Sam Lemon and Erin Light—were also absent.

Macleod thought he'd try to keep them away from the case as much as he could. They weren't based in Inverness, but in Glasgow, and to haul them up north and to see them around here would raise a lot of suspicion. The difficulty was that the Forseti group had a reach into law enforcement and Macleod wasn't sure quite where it got to. Sam and Erin had been great so far, but he didn't want to push it with them. After all, the team was still getting to know them.

'Morning, everyone,' said Macleod. 'Hopefully, you know why you're here now. I'm sure the rumour mill spoke to you as you arrived this morning.' With that, he glanced over at Clarissa. She wouldn't have been able to keep from telling Patterson.

'Everyone's aware to a point,' said Hope.

'Our Assistant Chief Constable has asked me to form a team to close the Forseti group down, and also what I'm calling the Revenge group—those the Forseti group have made a point of taking off the board. I've been told I can use any of you in any way I see fit. As you know, I run three teams: Arts team, Cold Cases, and the Murder squad. But as there will be two groups to go after, I'm going to put two of my inspectors in charge—one for each group. Clarissa will take the Forseti group. They seem to be steeped more in history and artefacts.

It'll suit her talents.'

He looked over at Clarissa, and instead of getting a barbed comment back, she simply nodded. He could tell she was nervous. After all, she had stepped back not so long ago to be an Arts team investigator. Here she was, back in the front line of murder.

'And the Revenge group will be taken on by Emmett. They seem to work out a lot of the shadows and I think Emmett's best suited to that. He's done well so far in unearthing a lot of this case. They'll keep their teams. So Patterson, you stay with Clarissa. Sabine, also with Emmett. However, Hope is going to be my second and run the dynamic between the teams. She'll hold the fort here.

'Hope will do some digging from here, and she'll also tie up how the two sides connect. Given Hope's pregnancy, I think it's unwise she's out there on the field, and she's in agreement. Otherwise, she'd be at the forefront of this. Let me make that clear. But as our most senior detective inspector, it's good that she has a helicopter view of it all to assist me. I'll switch to where I need to be.'

There was silence in the room, which was not normal when Macleod briefed. Usually there was the odd bit of banter, especially from Clarissa, but there was a sullenness to everyone there.

'Hope won't need a team here. There'll be plenty of people she can use for her tasks, so her team's going to split up. Clarissa, take Ross. You've worked with him before, closely. Susan, Perry and you are going to be with Emmett.'

'Is anybody else going to be involved?' asked Clarissa suddenly.

'How do you mean?'

CHAPTER 01

'Well, you know, anybody else coming in to help the team?'

'Sam and Erin are to stay in Glasgow and run things down there,' said Macleod.

'I wasn't talking about Sam and Erin. I was talking about our friends.'

'Kirsten will be about,' said Macleod. 'Anna Hunt is also working away in the background. You won't be connected with her directly. Hope and I can do that. But obviously, you may see some of her people about. You also may see Kirsten about.

'Be under no illusions. The threat at the moment to ourselves and families is high. And it is one reason I am determined to get this ended as quick as I can. Thanks to Perry and the rest of you, three young babies are today still with their mothers. We don't want that situation again. There are too many bodies behind us already. It's time to end it. No stone unturned. Push hard but watch your backs. Don't get caught out alone.

'These last few cases have told us that these people are killers. And they will kill you as much as anyone else. Be careful. Be very careful. Anything from home that seems strange, report it in. Send it to Hope. If you need to get a message to me, use Hope. If you can't get Hope for any reason, you can message through Tanya, but be aware that Tanya does not know most of what's going on. I'm doing that to protect her.'

'So where do we go?' asked Clarissa. 'How do we start this, Seoras?'

'The Forseti group we know operates in closed units. The Revenge group brought this out to us. Our link at the moment to the Forseti group is Bairstow. Yes, the Revenge group went after him, but he's still there. The chain wasn't cut. They didn't close him down straight away, and I believe he may be higher in this than we can imagine. Therefore, you get on to him, Clarissa. I want to know what he does, where he goes. I want to see how he contacts the group. Through him, we need to get to the top of the chain. We need to find out who runs it all. Only by taking off the snake's head are we going to close this down. Get an arrest. Make it public.'

'And for me?' asked Emmett.

'Hunt down the Revenge group. I want you to look into the arrested men, those picked up at Rogie Falls. Also, Emma Matthews. These men and Emma must have links to the group. They're not talking, but dig up everything about them. Chase it back through, Emmett. The links will be there, but they might be well hidden. Somebody is pushing this Revenge group from somewhere. Somebody is at the core. I want them, too. Remember, liaise with Hope. Go to your sections, make your plans, get out, get on with it. And remember, anything unusual, call it in. Take care of each other.'

'Did you say Perry was getting out today?' asked Emmett.

'Yes, and he'll want to come and work straight away,' said Macleod. 'Just watch what you give him. He's not a hundred per cent. In fact, he's probably about eighty-five. Give him something where he can put his brain to use, but don't put him into a melee. He's not fit for it.'

Emmett gave a nod and then stood up. He turned to Susan and to Sabine. 'Let's go.'

Clarissa stood, her team following her out, and soon the place was clear except for Macleod and Hope.

'You all right?' Macleod asked her.

'I'm itching to go there,' said Hope.

'I know. It's strange, though, having to let them go. I would have you running this,' said Macleod. 'You out in the field.'

'Things change,' said Hope. 'I don't work with you the same as I used to. You miss those days?'

'Those early days,' said Macleod. 'You and me, then Ross, then Kirsten. Yes, I do,' said Macleod. 'I do miss it. I don't have as much to teach you these days.'

'I must have done well then,' said Hope. She turned away to sit behind her desk and Macleod finished the last of his coffee. He took the cup with him as he exited and made his way back up the stairs towards his office.

'Oh,' said Tanya on seeing him, 'just had a call from the Assistant Chief Constable reminding you of the meeting this afternoon.'

Macleod wondered what that was, shook his head and looked over at Tanya.

'Budget meeting.'

Macleod nodded. Everything else would have to keep going, wouldn't it? Everything else would have to seem normal. He gave a grimace and entered his office.

Chapter 02

'Are you all right, Pats?'

'Of course, I'm all right,' said Patterson.

'I have let you drive,' said Clarissa.

'You've only let me drive because going around in a small green sports car brings attention. And you don't like this car, this . . . whatever you would call it.'

'Station wagon,' Clarissa spat. 'There's no class about it.'

'And clearly you wouldn't be in it, which is the whole point.'

'I meant,' said Clarissa, 'are you okay with Ross being on board? You've suddenly got a sergeant between us.'

'Sam's a sergeant.'

'But this is Als. I used to work with Als. Als and I used to be hand in hand back when he was a constable.'

'I'm fine with it. Needs done. We need him on board.'

'I've put him onto looking into Bairstow's affairs,' said Clarissa, 'because it's what he's good at. He's really good at computers. Getting in and finding stuff that's just sitting there in the . . . what do they call it? The net. The cloud. Cloud. The—'

'The net, cloud, whatever,' said Patterson.

'Yes,' said Clarissa. 'And you're here because you and I need to get closer to this guy.'

Bairstow had an estate to the northwest of Inverness, and Clarissa and Patterson had already tangled with him. Now, however, they were watching him from a distance. But Clarissa wasn't happy.

'The last time we were out checking on him, do you remember the security? I swear it's doubled at least, if not more.'

'That's hardly surprising,' said Patterson.

'No, Pats, it's not. But we have to get in there and work out how to tail him. How are we going to do that?'

'Let's work out what we can get,' said Patterson. 'We need to get his calendar. We need to work out where he's going to be.'

'How do we do that then?' asked Clarissa.

'Well, maybe we can get him to come to something, or coax him into a public event.'

'What? Just ring him up?'

'No, no, don't just ring him up,' said Patterson.

'Well then, Pats, what are we meant to do?'

'Well, we need to be subtle about it. We can't phone up as a company or that, because they could check it out.'

'So, what do we do?' said Clarissa. Patterson could tell she was getting agitated. His boss was sitting in what she considered to be not a very nice car and was fumbling around for ideas.

'Let's work out his diary by phoning up as the press, looking for an interview or whatever.'

'Better than that,' said Clarissa. 'I like the idea, but better than that, why doesn't somebody go in and talk to his people. Get a look at the diary.'

'Who?' asked Patterson.

'Well, you know how to hold a pencil and a notebook, don't

you, Pats?'

Patterson glowered at her. Clarissa told him to start the engine and get back to the station. There, they met Kirsten Stewart. In the space of an hour, she transformed Patterson, changing his hair, even his eyebrows, and the colour of his eyes. She couldn't do much about his height, but by the time he walked out of the office, Patterson looked positively ten years younger. Quite hip, as Clarissa would have thought of it, and now he smoked. He'd never smoked in his life.

Patterson took a car out towards the Bairstow estate, and on arrival, he made directly for the main entrance. He was stopped at the gate and approached by security. With the window rolled down, Patterson sat in the car, puffing away on his cigarette. He flicked the ash out through the window as the security guard came round to talk to him.

'I wish to speak to Lord Bairstow,' said Patterson.

'He's not available,' said the guard.

'Well, they need to make him available. I need to get time with him. They're going to do a big article, and he will not want to miss it. They're going to get syndicated out. It'd be good for him.'

'I don't think you want to be talking to him. I can get you to the press office.'

'He's got a press office?'

'That's only a couple of people, but you know, people who look after his affairs. He's got a lot on the go with his companies and that,' said the guard. 'It's the place for you to start, and the only way you'll get near him for an interview. Who do I say is calling?'

'James, James Cameron,' said Patterson.

'Just wait there,' said the man. Patterson continued to smoke,

CHAPTER 02

sitting in the car until eventually the guard came back. 'Go up to the house. We'll take you through from there. Don't barge in, just wait at the door, and Stephanie will be along in a minute.'

Patterson thanked the guard, drove up to the front of the house, and sat inside his car until Stephanie appeared at the door. He assumed it was Stephanie. She was tall, blonde, possibly in her thirties, and certainly looked efficient. He walked over, wiping a grubby hand on the back of his trousers before shaking hands with her.

'James Cameron. I've got a link to do quite a significant piece to get syndicated. I was hoping to interview Lord Bairstow.'

'What sort of piece are you thinking of doing?' she asked directly. 'And have you got guarantees it is happening?'

Patterson produced a letter that Kirsten had written for him. It explained how a magazine company would put it out amongst all of its productions. Stephanie seemed quite interested and turned, telling Patterson to follow her. As he did so, down what was a small corridor, he suddenly saw Lord Bairstow coming the other way.

'Don't forget, Stephanie, we want some press at the golf.'

'Of course,' said Stephanie. Patterson went to step forward, to shake hands with Lord Bairstow and say who he was, but Stephanie quietly moved him away.

'Don't forget,' said Stephanie, 'You don't speak to Lord Bairstow until I green light this. However, I think we can set up a preliminary meeting,' she said, as Patterson watched Bairstow walk away. He'd been within about three feet of Patterson and didn't seem to have clocked him at all for who he really was.

'When's he available?' asked Patterson as he entered the

office, pulling out a notebook.

'Well, we can have a pre-brief, let's say, a week on Tuesday. After that—'

'They'll want it out quicker than that,' said Patterson.

'Well, he can't do it this week. He's got a golf tournament coming up, down at the Oaks course.'

'All right, I guess that's it. I'll have to wait then. Guess I'll tell them I have to reschedule the timeframe. We can get it done a bit after that.'

Patterson made plans for six weeks' time when he would come for a pre-briefing and an exploratory talk about the interview. He, of course, had no intentions of being there for that. He would phone up and cancel, saying that the magazine had changed their mind. But this golf tournament sounded big.

Back at the station, Patterson explained to Clarissa about the Oaks golf course and the do that was coming up. Clarissa called Frank, her partner, asking him to find out some more details. Frank was a greenkeeper at their own local club and had contacts in the golf world. It was only a half an hour later when Frank called back.

'Hi,' said Clarissa. 'Did you get the information?'

'Yes, yes,' said Frank.

'Well, what is it?' asked Clarissa.

'Golf tournament down at the Oaks. It's a big do. The catering's coming in from outside. Ticketed. There are a few charities involved in it, too. I'd say you should look through the breast cancer lot. I think we've got contacts there. You know Marjorie?'

'Yes,' said Clarissa. 'You think Marjorie can get tickets?'

'Well, there's quite a lot of them going. She might get you in, if that's what you want to do. She'll tie you into the committee for a while, though. Depends if it's worth the price.'

'Well, I'll talk to her then about it. That's good, Frank. Listen, I don't know what time I'm going to be back for tea tonight, but if you want, get yourself a takeaway, and I'll get there when I can.'

'Right,' said Frank.

Clarissa got the feeling that Frank wasn't paying attention. It was unusual, because she'd asked him to do something for her and when it came to the police work, he pepped up. He usually was quite keen to talk about it.

'What's wrong?' she said.

'It's probably nothing,' said Frank.

'What's nothing?' asked Clarissa. Macleod had been warning them consistently to watch their backs. She would not take anything for granted.

'The last few times I've been up at the club and I've gone into my locker, well, there's been like this circle of stones.'

'A circle of stones,' said Clarissa.

'Yes,' said Frank. 'I mean, it's crazy. It's like there's a mini circle of stones in my locker.'

'What does it look like?'

'Well, it's a circle, isn't it?' said Frank. 'I don't get it. Why would you put a circle of stones down? It's weird.'

'How are the stones arranged?' asked Clarissa.

'Well, they've got an outer ring, and then at the centre there's this other stone in the middle.'

'And all the others have focused in on it?' asked Clarissa.

'Yeah, that's it. How did you know that?'

Clarissa suddenly felt her heart pound. They'd found a stone circle at Heligoland, the one that Forseti followers had used, and this seemed to be similar.

'Frank, did you, by any chance, get a photograph of it?'

'I did.'

'Can you send me that photograph?'

Five minutes later, Clarissa was looking at an image on the screen of the stone circle left in Frank's locker. It was clearly miniature, but it wasn't as if somebody had come in and just placed stones. These were glued down onto a base, and the stones were cut. The detail was crude, but the positions of the outer stones and the stone in the centre were accurate when compared to the Heligoland circle.

Clarissa swallowed hard as she phoned Frank back. She didn't want to worry him, but she made a check on what he was doing that day. He would be up at the club, as usual. That's what he usually did when she was working hard.

After telling him to take care, Clarissa made her way up the stairs of the station and into Macleod's office. She didn't wait for him to say come in. By now, Tanya had got to the point that unless Macleod was in with somebody, she just didn't stop Clarissa.

Macleod looked up as Clarissa arrived. 'So we've just abandoned all courtesy then,' said Macleod. He watched Clarissa slap a printout of the photograph sent by Frank onto his desk.

'That looks like Heligoland, the circle. Where did you get that from?' asked Macleod.

'That was inside Frank's locker,' said Clarissa.

'Up at the golf club?' asked Macleod.

'Not the first one, either. He says it's happened twice now.'

'Has he said anything else? Has he noticed anybody?'

'I'm trying not to spook him. He would have said if he'd

noticed somebody. Frank's not one to hold back.'

'Well, that's different,' said Macleod.

'I don't care if it's different. What do we do? Pull him out of there. That's a threat. That is a threat!' said Clarissa.

'From which side, do you think?' asked Macleod.

'Well, how much do the Revenge side know about these circles?'

'True,' said Macleod, 'but they could do. Of course the Forseti group revere these circles.'

'Do I need to take him to ground? Do I need to hide him? Do we need to hide all our people?'

'No,' said Macleod. 'Get back to work. I'll deal with it.'

'You'll what? You'll just deal with it? What are you going to do—invite him over for dinner?'

'Trust me on this,' said Macleod. 'I will deal with it. Frank will be safe. You go find me the Forseti group.'

Reluctantly, Clarissa turned away. And once she left the office, Macleod picked up his phone and dialled a number.

Chapter 03

'Do you think this office is going to work with four of us in it?' asked Emmett.

'It's going to be cosy. I guess we could ask Hope if we can use hers.'

'No,' said Emmett. 'Maybe it's best if we let Perry and Susan work from their own desks. They can come over here.'

'When's he coming out, anyway?'

'I sent Susan to pick him up,' said Emmett. 'Told her she can brief him on the way over in the car. Anyway, how are you getting on looking into the background of these men?'

'I've pulled the records of all three of them,' said Sabine. 'It's taken a while since their arrest at Rogie Falls to get full details on them, but it looks like we have it now. Their family history is interesting because they're all linked to Stu McIntosh's gang.'

'Well, that's not really unexpected, is it?' said Emmett. 'I thought he would be at the heart of it.'

'Yes, but they're all linked by their parents. It seems to be some sort of coming together, a reunion in the form of descendants—this Revenge group.'

'Well, the Forseti group took out many people from Stu McIntosh's gang,' said Emmett. 'They killed a lot of them. It's no wonder the McIntoshes are coming back at them. Glasgow seems to be the place where this happened. It's quite funny, having seen some of it up around Inverness and further out in Pitlochry.'

'Well, it's funny you should say that. One of our men has a sister called Belinda Macritchie. The men are locked up here, and their connections into McIntosh's gang or any other gang are difficult to see. They don't have criminal records. However, their parentage has linked them back to those who were in McIntosh's gang,' said Sabine. 'So, I thought maybe it's worth having a look at this sister.'

'Is there anything to say that she's involved?' asked Emmett.

'Well, the thing is, she's been recently tagged by Uniform here for snooping on a factory in Nairn.'

'A factory in Nairn?'

There was a rap at the door, and Susan squeezed into the small office, followed by Perry. His arm was still in a sling.

'Good morning, boss,' said Perry as he arrived. 'It's only temporary.'

'Are you fit to go, though? Macleod said you were not really fit to be running around.'

'The shoulder's going to take a couple of weeks. I don't really want to get into a fight,' said Perry.

'No,' said Emmett, looking at him. 'We could use your brains, though. There's a link we're investigating at the moment,' said Emmett.

He went to wave Perry and Susan to sit down, but then realised that he was a seat short. Susan slid onto Sabine's table, and Perry sat down.

'Sabine has linked a woman called Belinda Macritchie to one of the men we're holding. She's the sister, and their parents were linked to Stu McIntosh's gang. Apparently, she's been done for snooping on a factory near Nairn.'

'What factory?' asked Perry.

'Stow Beverages.'

'Stow Beverages?' said Perry. 'That's come up before when we were looking at Bairstow. Nothing sinister, but one of his companies.'

Sabine typed something into the computer. 'That's right. He's spot on. I guess we should look into that.'

'Tell you what we'll do,' said Emmett, 'Sabine, I want you out to tail Belinda. Find her here in Inverness, wherever she is. Stick on her.' He looked up at Perry and Susan. 'You worked down in Glasgow, didn't you, Perry?'

'Before I came up here, several years.'

'Good,' said Emmett. 'Go to Glasgow and get me some history on Belinda Macritchie. The McIntosh group got hit hard by the Forseti group. So, if our arrested people are linked back to them, as well as Matthews, what's to say that the McIntosh family isn't at the heart of this Revenge group?'

'We haven't been able to link the McIntoshes to leading the group yet, have we?' asked Perry.

'No,' said Emmett, 'but Macleod told me to use your brain. Get down there, find out what you can. Don't put yourself in any trouble. Susan goes with you. I'll take it you can handle yourself, Susan.'

'Always,' said Susan. 'I'll take care of him; don't worry.'

'Well, we'll not hang about then,' said Perry. 'I need to go home, get some packing done and take stuff down with me.'

'No risks,' said Emmett. 'Keep a distance. And find me the links.'

Emmett watched Perry and Susan leave and then saw Sabine

smiling at him.

'What?'

'Made her day,' said Sabine.

'How?' asked Emmett.

'Do you realise the fight that's going on for Perry at the moment?' Emmett looked bewildered. 'Perry is being chased down by two women, Tanya and Susan.'

'I don't care what he's doing with his love life.'

'Maybe not, but what you've done is put Susan alongside Perry, miles away from Inverness. Tanya will not be happy about that.'

'I don't care how they get their kicks at the moment, as long as it doesn't impede the investigation.'

'I guess it would be strange having somebody in the force that you're going out with. Do you think that would work?' asked Sabine.

'Who knows,' said Emmett. He stood up and turned to the filing cabinet, and Sabine sat there wondering why she'd asked that question. She looked at Emmett and felt such an immense surge of pride. Macleod had picked him out to run this side of the investigation, above everyone else. That was a lot, but Emmett was up to it. She was sure of that.

She stood up and grabbed her jacket. 'I'll get going then. I'll keep in touch. Will you be coming out to join me at some point?'

'I want to see what way it goes,' said Emmett. 'I'll try to do a bit more digging on these other men. See if we've got any more links.'

Sabine left the building and took a few hours to hunt down an address for Belinda Macritchie. Uniform had an address, but it was the afternoon before Macritchie came home, confirming it was there the woman lived. When she'd done so, Sabine followed her all evening. Belinda sat drinking in a pub with some friends before heading back to her house. It was the following morning when Emmett arrived.

'How's it going?' he asked.

'Well, she had some drinks last night. She's come back from work. I'm just going to see where she works today, hopefully. I'm struggling to find her employment. She can clearly afford a flat for herself,' said Sabine, sitting outside it in the car. 'I need to find out how.'

'Well, I can't stop with you,' said Emmett. 'I'm off checking out another connection. I'll tell you if it comes to anything. Let me know later how you get on.'

Emmett disappeared, and Sabine looked down at the front passenger seat of the car. There was a flask now with sandwiches and a hot bacon roll. She looked out of the car and watched him get into his and drive off. As he passed her, she gave him a smile through the window.

Sabine wondered if Emmett would do this for anyone in his team. Or was it just for her? She hoped it was just for her. He was funny. He didn't talk about romance at any point. Nor did he talk to her like she was some sort of potential partner. But he laughed in her company. He was open in her company and talked about things in her company he didn't do with the others. And yes, often those were the geekish things he was into. His board gaming, the miniatures that he painted. Emmett talked to her in a way he talked to no one else. She gave her head a shake.

'Get with it,' she said to herself.

Around about nine o'clock, Belinda Macritchie drove her car out to an industrial estate before parking up. Sabine drove

CHAPTER 03

by, then walked past, looking at the office she'd gone into. 'Highland Events,' a sign said. Sabine made her way back to her car and sat there watching while she took out her laptop and searched for 'Highland Events.' They'd been going for years, and basically were the people you called in when you needed either catering or entertainment for an enormous event. Sabine wondered exactly what Belinda's job was, and she decided she would need to pay a visit. Although she'd change her appearance first.

Entering the building, Sabine found a small reception desk and many people working at desks beyond. Sabine wore a hat to hide her hair, which was pulled up underneath it. She was dressed in a smart white blouse and skirt rather than the jeans and t-shirt she'd been wearing in the car.

'Hello,' said Sabine. 'I'm looking to see if your services would suit a little function I'm running.'

'Of course,' said the woman. 'My name's Andrea and I'll help you today. What sort of event have you got planned?'

Sabine spoke about a wedding conference she was thinking of running and started asking Andrea what sort of services could be provided. There were catering and entertainment ranging from the physical, such as bouncy castles and large sumo outfits, to crazy golf, laser tag, and such like. However, Sabine wanted to know more. As she was standing there conversing, she saw Belinda Macritchie sorting out uniforms.

'Which outfits are you taking along to the Oaks?' asked Andrea suddenly to Belinda.

'I thought given it's such a large do, we should go for the special set for the catering staff. The ones with the gold braid on the jackets and trousers,' said Belinda.

'I don't think so,' said Andrea. 'Smart enough, only. You

23

don't want to look too smart. It tends to make the punters feel like they're underdressed. It's a golf do, not an evening with the King!'

Belinda nodded. Sabine tried not to take too much of an interest and instead kept asking about things that would happen at a wedding conference. Having finished the conversation, saying she'd have a think and get back to Andrea, Sabine left the building, returned to her car. She called through to Emmett, advising him of what she'd found out.

'You think her job is important, though,' said Emmett over his mobile. 'I mean, what can she do from there? It's not like a lot of the other jobs people are involved in. She can't procure weapons. She's giving people food and entertainment. I don't see how that's going to help this Revenge group. Maybe she's just an ordinary person. Maybe it's her brother that's tied up in it. Happens sometimes, doesn't it?'

'We won't know,' said Sabine, 'but what choice do we have? She'll be close to Bairstow at the event.'

'Well, she'll be attending the same event, but that doesn't mean close.'

'Have you got anywhere with the other men we arrested at Rogie?'

'We haven't got anywhere, Sabine. Hopefully, Perry can find out something about them when he's down in Glasgow. They were driving down most of yesterday.'

'They'll come good,' said Sabine. 'Don't worry about Perry. Macleod rates him.'

'You're right,' said Emmett. 'We need to just keep at this. We'll surveil Belinda for a day or two. If nothing comes of it, then we'll have to dig deeper into the others. It's not going to be easy to get stuck into them when nothing's actually happening.'

'No, it's not,' said Sabine. 'So, we need to take it easy. Don't get too overexcited. We need to wait for her to drop the ball.'

'It's difficult when things are so quiet between the groups.'

'It's not really the dynamic start to an investigation, is it?' said Sabine.

'Investigations rarely do start dynamically. You have to just plod through,' said Emmett.

In her car, Sabine nodded. But what she really wanted to do was to get out of the car and go for a walk. She hated this being cooped up. She was much more active than that. Deep inside, she hoped that Belinda Macritchie would be an important link and one that would get them out and about much more, rather than sitting watching from a car.

Chapter 04

Frank was bemused. He didn't understand why people were sticking stone circles inside his locker. Also, how were they getting in? What was the point? He'd asked some of his colleagues at the club, but they were none the wiser either. He'd told Clarissa, but she hadn't told him anything that he didn't know himself. She'd offered no explanation for the stone circle. A small model. And it had happened twice.

Frank was just glad that, right now, he wasn't in the clubhouse, and was heading out in his buggy to the fourteenth green. It was a par four, and as he looked down the fairway, he'd seen that he'd probably have enough time to examine the hole on the green before any golfers would reach the green. He might have to cut a new one and shift it because somebody had said that the damage around the hole was getting severe. It happened sometimes around the edge and the lip, usually because people didn't put the flag in properly, nicked the side of it. Anyway, he was out to have a look.

As Frank approached the green, he thought he saw what looked like stones. Getting a little closer and out of his buggy, he saw on the green was a circle of stones with one in the middle. In fact, it looked very similar to the ones in miniature that had been placed into his locker. He was going to have to clear this up. He looked back down the fairway. There were two lady golfers coming up the fairway. They'd be hitting their shots into the green soon. He'd have to be careful.

* * *

That was the target. Dead ahead, on the green. If he could take the shot now, the body would be found beside the circle. They'd get the message, and his job would be complete. He held up the handgun with the silencer on the end. Forty feet. An easy shot for someone of his calibre. *What was the man looking at?*

The gunman quickly adjusted his position, looked down the fairway, and could see two lady golfers coming. *No, no, no. We don't want that. Out here in the open with no one watching was the key.* He could wait. The important point was they should not see him fall. Initially, it would look like a collapse and facilitate his escape. He would bide his time for the moment.

* * *

'Fore!'

Frank turned to walk off the green as a ball thudded into it. The ball ran through to the back of the green and out into the rough beyond. A second shot was incoming, only this one crashed into the trees on the far side of the green. *Oh*, thought Frank. *At least I'll be able to talk to them as they come up here. Get rid of these stones.* He stood patiently waiting at the side of the green, watching as the ladies approached the green.

'Did you see the ball come through?' asked one.

'There's one through the back. I believe the other one

crashed into the trees over there.'

'Really?' said the other woman. She was dressed in rather neat trousers and a plain jumper, but had black hair that was tied up in a ponytail at the back. She looked in her fifties and gave Frank a smile as if she knew him, before walking off toward the bushes. The other figure with her was younger, maybe in her thirties. She wore leggings under a skirt, along with a polo shirt. However, the beanie hat on her head told the story of a rather chilly day, despite the time of year.

'What on earth's that?' asked the woman, pointing at the stones on the green.

'I don't know,' said Frank. 'It just was here, and I was going to shift them, and then I saw you about to hit in. Thought I'd better leave it for the minute. I'm hoping it hasn't damaged the green.'

'The stones don't look that big, do they? Did you say my ball went all the way over there?'

'Yes,' said Frank. 'I'll tell you what, I'll let you hit back on if the stones aren't in your way. I'll move it after you're clear.'

'Well, thank you very much,' said the woman. She made her way off to the back of the green and then hunted for her ball. Frank looked for the other woman, but she'd already disappeared into the trees.

* * *

What's he chatting to her now for? The ball's gone through the back. All she's got to do is go over there. There might be an opportunity, thought the gunman. *There might be a chance. If she goes to the back of the green and her other friend, wherever she's gone . . .*

He looked down the fairway. The woman was heading into

the rubbish, not far from him but she would be at a distance. *There's going to be an opportunity*, he thought. He steadied himself, lifting the handgun again with the silencer on the end. *Once I shoot, double back out through the woods, onto the path, follow it down, pick up the car just off the course*, thought the man to himself.

Now where were the women going? The younger one, he watched as she strode across the green, looking down at the little pile of stones he'd made earlier. It was a bit of a faff, if the truth be told. He'd had to go in and plant the small stone circles into the man's locker, not once, but twice. And now this calling card, or whatever it was, had to be left on the green when he dispatched the man. It made little sense, but the money was good.

Oh yes, he thought to himself. *She's going for it. She's going to the back of the green. Right.*

He shifted his position and looked for the other woman routing off the fairway into the trees. *She's gone. She's gone into the rubbish. This was the opportunity.*

The man braced himself, lifted the gun and aimed. For a moment, his target moved behind a nearby tree and the man eased down again. But then, seeing him appear from behind the tree again, he lifted his gun and once again prepared to shoot.

Gently now, he thought. His eyes flicked over to where the woman had now gone off the back of the green. Her back was to him. She was out of the way. The other one was out of the way. *Now was the time. Perfect time to do it. And then as he falls to the ground, hitting the green and causing the women to panic and run towards him, I can escape.*

Just a few more feet. Just a few more feet. That's all it would take.

Move back for me. Move back for me.

He suddenly felt something and then felt nothing. His body pitched down, landing heavily amongst the foliage below the trees. The gun fell from his hand. If he had maintained any sort of consciousness, he would have seen a black ponytail swishing behind a face that came down close to regard him. A hand came out, checking his pulse.

The woman with the black ponytail then scanned the green quickly before unzipping the golf bag that she was pushing on its trolley. If he had still been alive, the man would have felt himself being picked up and then stuffed inside the bag, before hearing a zipper closing again. He would have heard the trolley being pushed back a short distance, and then he would have heard the woman say to herself, 'Hmmm, it's quite far buried down. Do I take a sand wedge, throw it up, as those trees would block it, or do I punch an iron into the back of it. See if I can plop it out onto the green? What to do?'

* * *

Frank watched the younger woman disappear off towards the back of the green. He turned, looking for the other woman, and then heard what sounded like a thud. He looked towards the bushes. It was coming from the far side, but there shouldn't be anybody there. The woman who'd gone into the trees was farther down. Not far, but enough to not be her.

He wondered if she'd found her ball yet. He looked again, to see where the sound had come from, then shook his head. That was the trouble. Out here in the open, sometimes things happened. Things fell out of trees. Wandering people and animals caused branches to crack or stumbled, causing noises.

CHAPTER 04

You didn't see them; you just heard them.

Frank calmly stepped to one side of the green, as the younger woman at the back chipped her ball on, and he watched it roll maybe seven or eight feet from the hole. It was a reasonable shot, nothing spectacular. And he smiled as the woman approached the green with her putter. She seemed content with the shot.

He waited off the green until he heard a crash, and a white ball flopped over the front apron of the green and ran up towards the hole, stopping only a few feet short. The older woman who had gone off into the trees was now approaching, pushing her trolley up the side of the green before she stopped and looked.

'Why are there stones on the green? Looks like something of crazy golf,' said the woman, almost with disgust.

'I don't understand. Vandals or something,' said Frank. 'I don't know who's doing it.'

'Are you wanting a hand with getting rid of it?' asked the woman.

'No, no,' said Frank. 'I'll do it. I was just going to let you putt through and you clearly got close enough to not be bothered by where the stones are.'

'Well that's immensely kind,' said the woman. She tended the flag while her friend putted, missed, and then sank her putt on the next go.

The woman then dropped her own putt and turned to Frank. 'Par,' she said. 'I think that's been a pretty good hole all the same. Lively, certainly interesting. Found a bit of rubbish I didn't expect.'

Frank nodded. 'I'll get on with clearing this away. There isn't anybody coming up behind you, is there?'

'You've got at least two holes clear,' said the younger woman.

Frank watched the women disappear through the hedge and out to the next hole. He brought the buggy round to the side, picked up the stones, which were rather heavy, dropping them in, and then drove off back towards the clubhouse. At the rear of the clubhouse was an area, not exactly a dumping ground, but certainly somewhere he could leave the stones without them getting in the way.

It took him five minutes to do this, and then he popped inside the sheds, which contained the gardening equipment for the course. He saw the young lad who had come up from the college. He made him a cup of coffee before taking him through seed preparation and how to make sure you got good drainage on your green.

The young lad looked thoroughly bored, and Frank wondered if he actually wanted to be here. However, the lad gave him an excuse to sit on his bottom, drinking coffee while he spoke. Only after that did he disappear back out in his buggy, driving past the car park. As he did so, he saw the two women from earlier and they waved over at him. He stopped.

'Did you get your stones cleared?' asked the older woman.

'Yes,' said Frank. 'Again, very bizarre. They were actually quite heavy. I can't understand why vandals would be running around with them. I'm not sure if they were even stones from around here. None of that type. It's all very bizarre.'

'Still, you've got it clear now.'

'All the same, I might tell the police.'

'The police,' said the woman with the black hair. 'Really? Do you know someone in the police?'

'I do indeed. My partner's in the police. Quite high up. Detective Inspector.'

'Oh, really? That must be exciting for you.'

'Oh, no,' said Frank. 'I don't get to see any of her cases. Well, I saw one. That's because it happened at the club. That's how I met her.'

'My, my,' said the woman with the black hair. 'Imagine that. Things going on at the golf club. What does she do? Theft?'

'No, she's in the arts side of things, but she worked in the murder squad back then. There were actually murders going on around the golf club.'

'Over what?' asked the younger woman. 'The handicap system? What makes people kill in a golf course?'

'I don't know,' said Frank. 'It was to do with . . . well, it was higher up. The funding of the club and all that sort of stuff. Not something I was involved in.'

'Oh well,' said the woman. 'You get all sorts of things, everywhere, don't you?'

'Let me give you a hand with the bag there,' said Frank.

'It's quite okay,' said the woman with the black hair, but Frank was out of his buggy already. He made for the trolley and grabbed hold of the bag to put it into the boot of the woman's car. As he picked it up, he found it to be incredibly heavy. However, he wouldn't let it show, and lifted the bag up before depositing it into the boot.

'There's a fair weight in that bag. What have you got in there?'

'Too many golf balls. Too much of this, too much of everything,' said the woman with blonde hair. 'She carries everything. Never seen somebody for equipment like it.'

'You want to kick some of that out,' said Frank. 'Be easier for you going round.'

'Oh no,' said the woman with the black hair. 'I like to have it with me, you know, for safety's sake. Just in case I run into anything unexpected.'

Frank laughed. 'What are you expecting? Some sort of military invasion?' He turned, jumped into his buggy, gave the woman a wave, and drove off.

As he did so, he was watched by black-haired Anna Hunt, who closed the boot of the car now that Frank had put her bag in. Macleod had done well getting in touch with her, but it was a rather close-run thing. Her other colleague, the one that wasn't with them in the car park, but who had been out on the course watching from the trees, had alerted her to where the man was. But even so, it had been touch and go to get there on time. She hadn't realised that he'd wanted to take him out on the course. Still, it had worked, and she had the body with her for identification now as well.

Anna turned to her colleague. 'A good round overall, I'd say.'

Chapter 05

Macleod sat behind his desk, pouring through reams of paper to sign. He didn't understand how when everything went on the computer, he still had to sign things. But Tanya brought it in, he put his name to it, and Tanya took it away again. He was ready for anyone, please anyone, to come through that door right now.

And then there was a knock. The door opened, Tanya stepped in, and held the door open as Jim, the Assistant Chief Constable, appeared behind her.

'Assistant Chief Constable—,' began Tanya.

'Jim,' said Macleod, and then to Tanya, 'A couple of coffees, please.'

'Sorry to barge in on you,' said Jim. 'Are you busy?'

'No, I'm just signing the bits of paper that will get taken up to you to sign after me. So no, you're a welcome distraction.'

'I just thought I'd see how things are getting on.'

'Well, there are days . . .' said Macleod. He pointed to the seat in front of his desk, which Jim took.

Jim went to speak, but Macleod held up his hand. He waited for a couple of minutes until Tanya had brought coffee in and then returned to her desk outside the office.

'She doesn't know anything?' said Jim.

'Tanya knows the team has been brought together. She knows I'm on something special, but no, she doesn't know any of the details. And she knows she doesn't know that. I think it's safer for her.'

'Safer?'

'I don't want anyone getting the idea that my secretary understands or knows all about what I'm doing. She might know the timings of meetings and that, but with regard to cases, she needs to be seen as aloof. Not worth grabbing hold of. She hasn't got the protection or the instinct that some of the rest of them have.'

'And you think that'll be enough for the rest of them?'

'No,' said Macleod. 'That's why I've taken other measures.'

'So,' said Jim, 'how's it going?'

Macleod's phone rang. He went to ignore it, but glanced at the screen that said it was Clarissa calling. 'Excuse me a moment, Jim,' he said, and picked up the phone.

'Seoras, you're coming to golf.'

'What?' said Macleod. 'I don't golf.'

'Doesn't matter, it's a golf social, okay? Bairstow is going to a golf social. So, you're going to come as well. I've got us some tickets for the event. Now, he knows who you are, he knows who I am, so we'll go there quite openly, and we'll put some other people in less openly. We've been trying to tail him when he leaves the estate, but to be honest, he hasn't left much recently.

'I think he's spooked, but he is going to this golf social. If he hasn't been moving about much and hasn't been getting out, I think he may contact someone while he's there. It's a possibility, and I haven't got a lot else I can do at the moment.

I can't get onto the estate to check what's going on. I've got no reason to get onto the estate.'

'And what are you expecting me to do at this golf social?' asked Macleod.

'Be your charming self. It's all right, I'll be there with you, so it's not like you're going to look as drab as normal. You'll have the colour beside you.'

'Can't you go on your own?'

'Of course not. The tickets I've got, the access I have procured, demands somebody pretty special. I hate to say it, but you command more of that than I do with your current status. You're practically a celebrity.'

'Never call me that,' said Macleod.

'Well, whatever. Just make sure you're available.'

'Why? When is it?'

'It'll be tomorrow night. You might want to wear a kilt.'

'A kilt,' said Macleod. 'When did I ever wear a kilt?'

'I'm just saying you could try to look a bit classy. You don't want to be outdone by me. Don't worry, I'll drive you there.'

'You want me to wear a kilt and go in that car?'

'Absolutely,' said Clarissa. 'I'll speak to you if I get anything else.'

Macleod put the phone down and Jim looked over at him.

'It's Clarissa,' said Macleod. 'She's getting me to go to a golf function tomorrow night, and insisting I wear a kilt.'

'You just good friends, or—?'

'No, no, it's to do with the case. Bairstow hasn't left his estate for a while. Now he's going out to this golf show, so he doesn't seem to want to cancel it. We're going along to watch him. He might speak to somebody there, make contact.'

'So anyway, give me an update,' said Jim.

Macleod's phone rang again. He looked over at it, then shook his shoulders at Jim before picking up the phone.

'Hope,' said Macleod. 'Do you really have to call?'

'I am a pregnant woman,' said Hope. 'I don't enjoy climbing the stairs at the moment. Starting to, well, yes, feeling it more than I did.'

'Of course,' said Macleod suddenly. 'What is it you need?'

'I've had Anna Hunt on the phone. She's . . . er . . . been in contact with Clarissa's Frank.'

'Clarissa's Frank?'

'Yes,' said Hope. 'You know he was getting stone circles left in his locker, but then there was one on the green. A man was out by the green when Frank was there and was going to take a shot at him. Anna Hunt killed him. She's taken the body away. Says he's a professional hitman. Won't get a link to the Forseti group, though they probably hired him. He's definitely a professional hitman. I reckon that might have been to make sure we can't trace it back to anyone. These kinds of hitmen, you don't discover their clients from them. Not sure Anna can get much more from the incident.'

'Is Frank okay?' asked Macleod.

'Anna said Frank was none the wiser. He even helped Anna put the body into her car. Not that he knew about it, however that works.'

'And Anna's suggesting what?'

'Anna's suggesting full protection for all our families. Guess it was kind of lucky that she found out about the stone circles and that.'

'Anna knew about them because I told her,' said Macleod. 'It wasn't luck at all. I was worried this was going to happen. They'll start coming for our other halves. Better make sure

John's warned. And contact Anna and tell her every bit of protection she can offer, I'm willing to take.'

'Do you want me to tell everyone else what's happening?'

'Probably not. It seems contrary to best practice, but it's usually better if she works in the dark with her people and we don't know them. They'll be there if needed. The more we put on our people, the more they're all going to worry. They'll be worried enough with this case.'

'Very good,' said Hope.

Macleod put the phone down and turned back to Jim. He reached over and grabbed his coffee, took a drink of it, before settling back down again.

'Who was that then?' asked Jim.

'That was Hope. Fortunately, I was able to prevent Clarissa's partner from dying.'

Jim looked at him, and Macleod shook his shoulders. 'He was getting stone circles put in his locker. I assumed it might be the Forseti group up to no good. And I told Anna Hunt. Anna has dispatched a professional hitman who was trying to kill Frank. There'll be no investigation as she discreetly put him out of the way. But she said he's professional, and he's unlikely to give a lead back into the Forseti group.'

'That could have been a good line in.'

'I've asked Anna to run protection for everybody.'

'We could do police protection,' said Jim.

'I'd rather not,' said Macleod. 'We don't know how far the reach of the Forseti group goes. Therefore, I think the idea that it's run by Anna Hunt, who I certainly do trust, is the better option.'

'As you will. So, what's happening with the rest of the case?' said Jim.

Macleod's phone went again, causing him to put his hands to his head. But then he saw it was Emmett and picked up, excusing himself to Jim.

'Emmett, what have you got for me?'

'Following up on Belinda Macritchie,' he said. 'She's got a job with an events organiser. We've been keeping a tail on her. We haven't found anything untoward with her at the moment. But she had that case of being lifted for snooping around Bairstow's property.'

'Well, we've all got to start somewhere,' said Macleod. 'Anything else?'

'I've sent Perry down to Glasgow, along with Susan. He tells me that Belinda Macritchie had been working at a men's club owned by Ellen McIntosh's family. Came across it when looking at her brother. So there's a direct link in. I'm not saying that the McIntoshes are behind everything, but there's a link there. And Perry says that Belinda was listed as a dancer at this club. Now, dancer means erotic dancer because it's a men's club. Strip joint,' said Emmett. 'Perry said that was all right, except that she didn't look like a woman who'd work in a strip club. Her size and shape were all wrong.'

'Well, what size and shape was she?'

'Slightly larger woman,' said Emmett. 'Perry said you don't get those sorts of women in strip clubs.'

'I wouldn't know,' said Macleod.

'No, I wouldn't either,' said Emmett.

'So, what's the plan?' said Macleod.

'Well, Sabine and I'll stay on Belinda. We'll see where she goes the next day or two. I've told Perry he needs to get closer to this strip club link. Find out what Belinda was doing down there. Find out who she's talking to. See if she's visited recently.'

'Just make sure you don't overexcite Perry,' said Macleod.

'Well, Susan's with him,' said Emmett, almost absentmindedly. 'I'm sure she'll be delighted going there.'

Macleod closed down the call and then relayed to Jim what Emmett had just said.

'If it's the McIntosh family,' said Jim, 'you may be in luck. Easy connections. And also, the Revenge won't run so deep if we pick them up.'

'We have one advantage,' said Macleod. 'The Forseti group doesn't know who it is that's coming after them. We don't either. But that means we're both hunting. If they find out before us, this Revenge group could be as good as dead for I don't think they'll hold back on them.'

'No, they won't,' said Jim. 'That's important to note.'

'Have you got any further,' asked Macleod, 'any idea who knows higher up? Ideas of anybody within the force working with the Forseti group?'

'I don't, but I haven't been talking to a lot of people about what's going on. It's only the Chief Constable who knows, especially about this task force I've given you. Just him, me, and you and your team. The trouble with that is if it goes public,' said Jim. 'If people find out about it, they'll really come hard down on you, try to eliminate you. At the moment, working in the dark, so to speak, keeps you safe.'

'Well aware of that,' said Macleod.

'Well, I'll get out of your hair,' said Jim.

He stood up, walked to the door, and then stopped and turned to Macleod. 'Take very good care, especially of Jane too.'

'Don't worry about that. I'll be looking after her,' said

Macleod. He stood up, watched Jim exit before turning and looking out of the window of his office. After a moment, he made his way downstairs to Hope.

She was not in her office. He went in anyway, decided to wait for a moment, and sat down. Soon after, Hope walked in, looking white.

'Sick again?' asked Macleod.

'You think at some point it's going to go away? Or am I just going to puke my guts for the rest of my life?'

'I take it everything's going okay, though?' asked Macleod.

'Apart from feeling like hell, yes.'

'How did Anna sound?' asked Macleod. 'I had Jim in earlier, so I didn't want our conversation to go on too long.'

'I think Anna's worried. It was close, apparently, with Frank, although he doesn't know it.'

'How do you feel about it, though?' said Macleod. 'Anna Hunt coming in, taking out a hitman, taking him away without touching this case.'

'On the bright side,' said Hope, 'it won't interfere in the case. I think we've got to be careful. We've got to be careful if we're going to arrest these people. They'll have significant resources, lawyers. They could be saved by any minor infraction. Anna coming in and doing this is good. This is Anna keeping us clean, so to speak, being helpful. Not my way of doing it, though.'

'Indeed not,' said Macleod. Macleod turned to walk out the door, and then he stopped and looked at Hope. 'I think I have to warn you, it's only fair,' said Macleod.

'What?'

'Perry with Emmett. I think Perry might jump ship permanently.'

'What do you mean?' said Hope.

'He seems to like the assignments he's getting.'

'Why?' asked Hope.

'Well, on day one, Perry's been sent to a strip club.'

'Get out of it!'

'I'm telling you, Emmett knows how to sort out his troops.'

Hope threw a pencil at him as he closed the door and Macleod heard it bang off the door to fall to the floor. You had to keep the humour going. You had to keep the laughter. But inside he was worried. They'd come for Frank. They could come for anyone.

Chapter 06

Emmett and Sabine had been tailing Belinda Macritchie for nearly two days now. In the late morning, they followed her from her work at the events organiser, through to a golf club on the outskirts of Inverness. The Oaks Golf Club had a rather grand clubhouse, and together Emmett and Sabine watched from the car park as Belinda and her colleagues began taking glasses, bottles, and many table decorations through. Belinda was dressed rather smartly, and it certainly looked like there would be quite a shindig that night.

'How do we play this?' Sabine said to Emmett. 'We can sit here, and we can watch as she goes and does her job. Or we can get in close to see if she's doing something while she's doing her job.'

'Maybe it's best to wait until later,' said Emmett. 'It's usually easier to maintain a disguise when everybody's busy. At the moment, it's steady. But when people arrive for this event, it's going to get a bit more chaotic. It's also easier to mingle amongst a bigger crowd.'

'Good idea,' said Sabine. 'But maybe I can get somewhere in the meantime. Get an outfit for this evening. I'll be back shortly.'

Sabine left the car and quietly began negotiating her way towards the inside of the clubhouse. The interior was dark in places. Corridors with photographs on the wall of former years of golf competition. These were once pride of place but were now resigned to back corridors heading to basements where alcohol and suchlike were stored.

As she walked through, Sabine found one room had been set up with lots of garments for servers. They had kilts hung there, along with waistcoats and white blouses. Sabine grabbed an outfit she thought would fit her. She disappeared back out with it under her jacket before getting into the car with Emmett.

'I think I can get in tonight,' she said.

'Well, if I watch from the outside and you watch from the inside, it's probably going to be easiest. You can call it if anybody leaves in a hurry or gets a message or something.'

'Good,' said Sabine. 'I'm tiring of sitting in the car.'

At half past six that evening, Sabine entered the clubhouse wearing a tartan skirt that was just a little higher above her knees than she would have wanted. The bow tie was slightly tight, but the waistcoat made her look smart. She had her hair tied up. Sabine wasn't quite sure what she should be doing. As she entered, she saw a tray of full wine glasses, picked it up, and walked through the large reception room of the clubhouse.

There were plenty of people there. Dignitaries, men in smart suits, women in elaborate dresses. It was only when she crossed to the other side of this wooden-floored room that she clocked two familiar faces. Standing holding a whisky was a purple-haired woman wearing a lady's kilt along with a white shirt and a tartan sash. There was a family brooch pinned on to the sash and she was chatting animatedly to several people around her.

Standing beside her was Macleod in a rather dull black suit. Unlike Clarissa, he spotted Sabine and gave her the faintest of nods.

Sabine quickly picked out Belinda Macritchie, wearing a similar outfit to herself, and also serving drinks. Sabine kept her distance. As she wheeled around with the drinks, Sabine passed by Macleod, stopping briefly beside him.

'Stand there a minute,' said Macleod, reaching up and taking an orange juice off the tray that Sabine was holding. He was glancing over her shoulder. 'Keep talking to me,' he said, 'nice and chatty.'

'I hope you're having a good time. How come I get to work, and you get an invitation? And what are you doing here, if you don't mind me asking?' said Sabine in a quiet voice.

'Bairstow's here. So, Clarissa has dragged me along. It's the first time he's been out in ages.'

'Well, Belinda Macritchie is here too. Along with the entertainment company she's working for.'

'That's interesting,' said Macleod. 'What's more interesting is Bairstow's over across the room behind you. And I swear he's just taken a message from someone.'

'What do you mean?'

'He's got handed something. Gently. It was good, very good. But I clocked it.'

'What are you going to do?'

'Clarissa, can you come here a minute?' Macleod called.

Clarissa smiled politely at the person she was talking to. She turned round to Macleod, with a rather grumpy face. 'What?' she said. 'Look, Sabine, I get him here and look at the state of him. What sort of an outfit is that to wear?'

CHAPTER 06

'Shush,' said Macleod. 'You having fun? I've just seen Bairstow handed a note.'

'So what are we going to do about it?' said Clarissa.

'It was handed by that gentleman there,' said Macleod, pointing very gingerly with his small finger so that nobody else could see. 'Get on to him, get a photograph of him, see if we can work out who he is.'

No sooner had Macleod said it, and Clarissa was marching her way across the hall, tracking the man who had passed the message.

'If she's here,' said Macleod, 'and you think she's up to something—'

'Bairstow's here,' said Sabine, 'so she could be here for him. I'll keep an eye on her.'

'No,' said Macleod. 'I'll keep an eye on her. She's got to be here serving. Her entertainment company brought crates of things, as my conversations have elucidated. If you're going to do something, you might have it with you. Go on through their operation. Go see if there's anything untoward. You'll be able to get in there with that outfit on.'

'Will do,' said Sabine.

'Where's Emmett?' asked Macleod.

'He's waiting outside.'

'Okay. If anybody comes out that I tell him about, he can tail someone in the car. Very good. Off you go. If you need me to cause a diversion at some point, come back and tell me. It won't be a problem,' said Macleod.

Sabine disappeared out one door and into one of the darker corridors that the staff were using. There were many hidden rooms within the golf club and equipment, clothing, extra food, and booze had been stored away there. Sabine stole into one room and started searching through different amounts of clothing and some boxes. Everything looked normal. There were cases of champagne there as well. She wondered how long before they would come out. There were boxes with extra glasses, as this do was clearly bigger than those the golf club normally held.

Sabine left that room, creeping into another one. Here there were more clothing racks and items to decorate tables with. Most of the boxes, however, were empty, with the decorations already being in use. Sabine kept going into a third room, and here she found a box pushed away to the back, hiding behind plenty of other ones. She made her way over and then stopped as someone else entered the room.

'Are you meant to be on drinks?' said a woman's voice.

'I'm on my break. I'm on my break,' blurted Sabine.

'How did you get a damn break? Everyone gets a damn break except me. Who did you talk to about the break? Christine? Is Christine the one running the breaks?'

Sabine nodded. 'Don't look at me. I just got told to go on a break and I'm taking it.'

The woman shook her head at Sabine and then disappeared back out of the room. Sabine quickly checked the box that was sitting on its own, away from the others. She opened it up and gasped. There was a gun there with a silencer on it. She looked at the edge of the box. Somebody had written in black marker pen 'rubbish.' And indeed above the gun had been a layer of what you could say was rubbish. Lots of bubble wrap. Sabine took out her phone and called Emmett.

'There's a gun here. It's come in with the entertainment company. Look, I've taken photographs and that of it. But in case it's going to be used, we need to get it out of commission.'

CHAPTER 06

'What are you suggesting?' asked Emmett.

'I'm going to wrap it in bubble wrap and I'm going to drop it out one of the windows. If you go round the back of the clubhouse, near the women's toilets, there's a small window up there. I'll drop it. You can put it in the car. Then at least it's out of commission. And when you've done that, I'm going to get close to Belinda, watch her and see if she comes back for the gun. She's bound to go for Bairstow at some point. It just seems so obvious.'

Sabine took the bubble wrap, wrapping up the gun, and placed it underneath her waistcoat. She walked down a couple of corridors before stopping at a small window. She cracked it open and dropped the gun out the back. It never hit the ground. Emmett was quick, and she thought of the gun being whisked away into the boot of their car.

Sabine re-entered the room, looking now for Belinda. She couldn't see her, and walked over to Macleod, casually picking up a tray of drinks to offer him when he shook his head.

'I thought you were watching Belinda,' she said.

'Where's she gone?'

'She disappeared out with an empty tray of drinks, and she hasn't come back,' said Macleod. 'Kind of hard to follow her.'

'Well, I found a gun in amongst the boxes from the entertainment company.'

'You think she was here to use that? Maybe she's done a runner then, maybe she's—'

'Emmett's outside. He would have said. He's got the gun though. We'd better find her.'

Meanwhile, Sabine could see Clarissa at the far end of the room. There, the man she'd been pursuing was standing with her and having a selfie taken of him.

'It's an absolute delight to meet you,' said Clarissa.

'Thank you. Thank you for sharing that.' She came back over towards Macleod, beaming. 'There you go. Got a selfie of our man. Lovely close-up photograph. I'm sure we'll be able to get him from that.'

'I'd rather find out what the note said,' muttered Macleod. 'That would really help us.'

'Have you seen Belinda?' asked Sabine.

'No. I thought you were watching her,' said Clarissa.

'I had to do a check. There's a gun that came in with the entertainment company. One of their boxes. Emmett's got it now in our boot, out of the way.'

'You think somebody's come here to shoot?'

'Seems like it,' said Sabine, 'but I can't find Belinda at the moment.'

As the three were standing together, they heard screaming. A young woman, maybe only eighteen years of age, came racing into the room. She was dressed in a rather fancy cocktail dress and when she ran, her high heels caused her to stumble. She entered the room almost tripping on her own feet before she did indeed slip and hit the wooden floor hard. Her eyes were full of tears already, though.

'Easy, love! What's up? You okay?' said a rather jovial man in a kilt.

'She's dead!' the girl shouted. 'She's dead!'

'Oh, it can't be as bad as all that,' said the man in the kilt, which shocked Macleod because there was no evidence that everything was okay.

'She's in the women's changing rooms, down there.'

Macleod stepped forward. Sabine wanted to help, but given her current outfit, it wasn't something she could do without

CHAPTER 06

giving away her position.

'I'm a police officer,' said Macleod, bending down to the young woman. 'Tell me what you're talking about. What's happened?'

'Women's changing rooms,' said the woman, tears pouring from her eyes. 'She's there.'

Macleod turned and told Sabine to look after her, showing Sabine was just part of the staff. He then strode, followed by Clarissa, down some corridors before arriving where there was a small contingent hanging outside. He brushed past them inside the changing room. There was a small fan at the top. Hanging from it, attached by a necktie, was Belinda Macritchie.

Macleod grabbed her legs, pushing her up. 'Check for a pulse, see if she's still alive,' he told Clarissa. Clarissa pulled a chair over and stood up on it so she was able to reach to feel the woman's neck. She undid the tie, and, along with Macleod, laid her down on the floor. Other people were coming into the room, and Macleod turned, shouting at them for a doctor.

'Everyone here, if you're not a doctor, get out and stay out!' said Macleod. He reached down, but he couldn't find a pulse. Macleod began CPR. He wasn't particularly good at it, but it needed to happen.

Clarissa put a phone call in for an ambulance. As she did so, she saw Bairstow momentarily entering the changing rooms, before disappearing back out again. This wasn't unusual in the sense that plenty of people were trying to get in to see what was going on. Most on finding out the situation were disappearing back out, worried they might be asked to do something.

It took the ambulance fifteen minutes to arrive. As Macleod stepped back, the paramedics took over. He sat down in the corner of the changing room, Clarissa beside him.

'Bairstow was looking very nervous when he was in here,' said Clarissa.

'He needs to get more than nervous.'

'Are you all right?' asked Clarissa.

'Just like that. Dead. Just like that, taken out. Makes little sense. If she was here to get him, if she was here to kill him, how did she just end up so easily—'

'I don't know, but I'll tell you something. When Bairstow came in, he looked nervous, very nervous.'

'You think it's the girl?' said Macleod. 'Or the note?'

'You tell me, Seoras,' said Clarissa. 'You tell me.'

Chapter 07

The sun had barely risen over the surrounding mountains when Hope pulled up alongside the shore of Loch Ness. Even at this time, she could see holidaymakers out and about, though not in so great a number as to make it inconvenient. Hope had been up since four thanks to her now seemingly obligatory run to the bathroom. The morning sickness wasn't abating and part of her just wanted to get this baby out. The trouble was, she hated herself for saying that when she looked down and saw the bump had grown. Not to a point where she waddled, but you could certainly tell she was a pregnant woman, even without looking at her hair.

Hope sat down on a wooden bench and looked out at the water. There was a light breeze, and the surface rippled, but it looked peaceful. It was everything the investigation wasn't. People were dead on a hard path to tread to get access to the players.

Part of her wanted to be out there amongst it, but she knew she couldn't, not with this little one on board. Macleod had kept her in the loop. She hadn't been looking to even do that. She wasn't sure he needed her. Or was Seoras keeping her alongside because he was worried about her, from a protection angle? If she'd gone off on maternity, would he be able to have the same connection, be able to have the same people watching over her? There were people watching, weren't there? They were watching John, certainly.

Hope wasn't sure how she did it, but Anna Hunt appeared less than fifty yards away. She shouldn't have been able to do that. Hope should have seen where she had come from. One moment, the woman was not there, the next, there, bold as brass.

'That is some head of hair you have now,' said Anna. 'Makes me jealous. Always wondered how mine would go if I ever had a child. Won't know now.'

'They always say there's time, don't they? Look at all these celebs. Being a late mother is the thing these days.'

'I think I'm a little late for that.'

Anna had a small bag over her shoulder, and she placed it down on the bench between them.

'I usually bring Macleod a coffee. I wasn't quite sure what to bring you. Got some hot water. There's decaf coffee, decaf tea, peppermint. There's even some raspberry there. They say it's good for relaxing things. I wouldn't know, though.'

'Decaf coffee's fine,' said Hope.

She sat back in the chair while Anna made the coffee and then handed Hope a cup. Hope took it, sipped on it, and looked up and down the loch. Loch Ness was a kind of paradise at the moment. Flowers were in bloom. You could hear the bees. There was a life to the loch that was missing in the early months of the year. It was still wonderful in its own way then—stark, but almost foreboding.

'Anyone ever get the wrong idea about Seoras and you?' said Hope. 'Sitting out here, when you meet up.'

'Who said it was the wrong idea?'

Hope shot a glance towards Anna and gave a smile. 'Who knows? He's got a partner,' said Hope. 'Seoras is not that sort of guy.'

'I know,' said Anna, almost resigned. 'And so do you. You knew it quite early on, didn't you?'

'What are you talking about?'

'Something about him, isn't there? And you'll have thought, he's significantly older, and it's not really something I should do, but if he'd offered, would you have taken the chance?'

'I'm not answering that,' said Hope.

'And I'm not answering anything about why I meet him out here in the loch, and about why it's such a pleasant, almost romantic place.' Anna glanced at Hope again with a smile that was wicked.

'Can we talk business?' said Hope. 'I'm a little more comfortable with that.'

'Of course,' said Anna. 'The man who was out to kill Frank was a hired gun. He was a good one at that.'

'He wasn't that good,' said Hope. 'He didn't succeed.'

'That's because he was spotted. He was good, but I'm better. My team was out and about managing surveillance, especially after Macleod's comments to us about the stone circle in Frank's locker. We'd spotted the man, and we'd watched him set up. Frankly, he spoiled a rather decent round of golf for me.'

'You were playing golf?' said Hope, surprised.

'Yes, easy way to be out there—no questions as you roam the course. We had one pair of eyes watching the shooter. Nearly lost him a few times. We were also watching Frank, too. As soon as they got anywhere close together, a colleague and I came in to help. I regret having to take the man down,' said Anna. 'It would have been better if we could have brought him in. But that type, they don't give out. They don't tell you about clients, right to the death. They can't. It's how they keep their business, their special brand. They know it's done when it's done. They check out calmly, quietly. If I'd have taken him into custody, he'd probably have killed himself.'

'So, we don't know who sent him.'

'Oh, it's the Forseti group, for sure. No proof though. The other thing is I've set up full protection on Frank, your John, Angus, Ross's partner, and Macleod's Jane. Tempted not to do that one. Potentially could have opened a gap in the market.' Hope looked shocked but Anna just smiled wickedly again. 'You would really think that of me?' she said. 'The trouble with coppers is they don't know when people are being serious.'

'I suppose you do,' said Hope.

'Kind of a pre-requisite for the job. If you don't know, you can end up with a brief career.'

'Basically, you're telling me you stopped Frank from getting killed—which I thank you for, and I'm sure Clarissa will, too—but outside of that, we have got nothing, except more protection.'

'I wouldn't write the protection off so quickly. It saved Frank's life.'

'Trust me. I'm not writing it off quickly. The idea you have people around John is a colossal relief to me.'

'Well, that's partly your own fault, isn't it?' said Anna.

'What do you mean?' said Hope.

'You could have walked away. Pregnant, off on maternity leave. I mean, then the force wouldn't have minded, would they? Your bosses would have been showing they were an equal opportunities employer. Generously, they gave Hope her time to go off and have her baby, then come back. You'll still be the pin-up if your figure remains the same. Who knows?'

'I'm not the pin-up,' said Hope.

'Can I speak candidly?'

'If you must,' said Hope.

'You are the pin-up. You were always the pin-up. Look at you, six feet, glorious body, magnificent hair, and that's not your fault. You were fortunate that you met Macleod. He was the one who brought you up. He sees beyond just a figure. They all talk about how many women he has on his team. They're all there for good reason. Not simply because they look good, not to make up the numbers. Not everyone works that way. Trust me, I'm jealous. I wish I had the looks to go along with the brains.'

'You're not doing bad though, are you?' said Hope.

'There'll come a time and an age when your looks won't be there,' said Anna. 'Not like they are now. And then you'll notice those men start to switch off. You don't get the same number of doors held open for you, don't get talked about, approached. With me, it was the doors. Maybe that's an age thing. I don't know what it will be for you, but you will when it comes.'

'Sounds bliss,' said Hope.

'No it isn't, because you can use that,' said Anna. 'You can use everything about you. And when some of these tools of your trade are gone, you have to work even harder. It doesn't get any easier.'

'Can we get back to the case, now that you've done an assessment of me?'

'In a moment. Be ready.'

'What?' blurted Hope.

'Be ready. Macleod will make way. He will make way for you.'

'What makes you say that?'

'He's already done it,' said Anna. 'Macleod doesn't want to be away from the front lines. He loves it. It's what makes him tick. And he's darn good at it. If he walked away and left you behind, he must think you're up to it. But be ready. It won't be that much longer before he calls it a day. I can hear it when I talk to him. Comes to us all, I guess.'

'Back to business,' said Hope, a little unnerved.

'Our shooter. I found a napkin on him. Came from Donato's. It's an Italian restaurant in Inverness.'

'I know Donato's,' said Hope.

'Well, the man had a cold, and he's wiped his nose on the napkin. So, he was there. Not something you'd bring along for later. Or get handed out and about. He must have been there. Now he's the guy coming in from beyond the Forseti group. So, Donato's may have been a safe place to meet. That will mean that they have used it before. Maybe even regularly. Could be there's a back room. Maybe there's somewhere else within it. I don't know. But that's your connection,' said Anna. 'Other than that, he was clean. I'm still trying to work out his real name.'

'Good,' said Hope. 'At least something's come from it.'

'I'll keep the protection in place. Don't worry, now I know they're coming for them, things will be easier. I'll also make sure their protection is obvious. If I do that, I doubt they'll come for your partners specifically.'

'Why?'

'Because if they do, they'll be invoking my wrath, and they

won't want to do that,' smiled Anna.

'You see, there's an arrogance that comes with being at the top, and it's one that's quite frightening. You believe you can take charge of anything, believe you're on top of it all. Understand, you're not,' said Anna.

'When you get to the top,' she continued, 'you have to dot all the "i's" and cross all the "t's", just the same as everyone else. The Forseti group will think of you as simple plods, police officers. Therefore, they should be able to control you. They'll be more wary if they think I'm involved. So, I will make my involvement about protection obvious. I'll make it known that Macleod has asked me for some help in that regard, not in any other. That way, you'll keep your loved ones safe. However, it won't stop the Forseti Group coming for you or the team, which could be an important asset.'

'An asset?' queried Hope.

'Secret societies don't move very often. Secret groups—they're tight. When they do, that's the chance to get inside of them, find out who they are, what they are. We scare them, and they will run. We'll never find them and they will still carry out what they want to do, because it's their raison d'être. They know how to operate in that way. At the moment, they're on new ground with how the Chief Constable has given Macleod a freer hand. That's why they sent a gunman, to scare you off. If they knew Macleod at all, they would know that this will drive him to go harder.'

'It will,' said Hope.

Anna stood up and looked down the loch. 'It is lovely, isn't it? Absolutely stunning. I envy you guys working up here, the mountains, a bit more of the wilderness. It may surprise you, but I don't enjoy London. I think that's why I'm away from it as often as possible. Anyway, take care of yourself, take care of that little one. I wish you all the best with it.'

Anna packed up her things in her bag. Hope finished her drink before handing Anna her cup.

'Some night you and I need to go out,' said Anna. 'Properly out. When you're not being a detective. Unwind a bit. Tell some stories.'

'I'd love that. But when's that going to happen?' said Hope. Anna laughed. Hope watched as Anna departed before picking up her phone and calling Macleod.

'What have you got?' said Macleod.

'Met with our friend. She says that our hitman ate at Donato's. There's a napkin with his snot on it. I think it's going to be our best chance. I'll investigate.'

'Whoa,' said Macleod. 'What happened to Office Hope?'

'It's just a restaurant. A mere stake-out.'

'We've got other people who can get involved in this. I'll give Emmett a call or Clarissa. Get them to do it.'

'No,' said Hope. 'Don't. You've got them off on their own tangent. They've got their focus. This is different. Let me take this.'

'I'm not sending you out on your own.'

'Just because I'm pregnant? I can drive myself about,' said Hope. 'It's not a problem.'

'No, it's because there's two dead already within the last week,' said Macleod forcefully. 'If you were fully fit, I'd send somebody with you.'

'Well, send somebody with me then.'

Hope could hear the deep sigh and resignation in his voice. But would he order her back to the office?

'Okay,' said Macleod, 'but it's reconnaissance only? Any

CHAPTER 07

trouble, you step back, you get away.'

'You don't have to tell me twice.'

'And I'm giving you Kirsten.'

'I thought Kirsten was going to be monitoring us, running around.'

'The genie's out of the bottle with the hitman. You've just spoken to Anna Hunt, and I'm guessing she told you she's going to run protection for everybody.'

'She did. She said they would look after John, Angus, Frank, Jane.'

'Exactly as I asked her to. She wants us investigating this. She'll make sure everything is in place, so we don't get unfocused. You're getting Kirsten, and you will listen to her when things go south.'

'I will listen to what she says.'

'No, Hope,' said Macleod. 'If she says it's too dangerous, you get out. I know what you're like. If you see the chance, you'll go for it, but not this time. Not this time.'

'When have I ever put too much at risk, Seoras?'

'You dived off the side of a dam into a river, and it was how high up?'

'Touché, Seoras. I'll bow to Kirsten's lead.' There was a grumble on the call. Hope wasn't sure he believed her. She wasn't sure she believed herself.

Chapter 08

Perry sat with a bottle of beer in front of him. Currently, he was struggling to believe that this was his work. In front of him, on a stage, was a young woman, maybe twenty-five years of age. She was jiggling this way and that, and giving Perry a view that was usually reserved for intimate partners.

Across the floor of the club were several other women, undressed in a similar vein, and enticing men with their dancing. Perry had already had three or four of them come up and asked if he wanted a private dance. He was in a quandary. He was working. And he was in a place that, frankly, Perry wouldn't visit.

Perry had to admit that the view wasn't unattractive. Many women wearing, well, absolutely next to nothing, and jumping about for his entertainment. What was not to like, he thought at first. But Perry found it cold.

Yes, the animal inside him was excited, almost enjoying itself. But Perry was more than just his animal side. Though a man, he also wanted a bit more than just what he could see. The detachment, the almost lack of passion, of tension, was killing the moment for him.

He was also wondering how he could explain that to any of his male colleagues. Maybe the female ones would understand how he thought for a moment. No, he wasn't discussing this with Susan, Tanya, or Hope, or any of the rest of them for that matter.

Perry's job was to determine which of the women in the club were actual dancers. He was to separate them from those coming to the club for secret meetings in the rear of the building.

He thought he'd done a good job, but in truth, it wasn't that difficult—at least not for some women. The job itself required you to have a certain look about you, and some women who came in didn't have that. He'd almost decided who was and who wasn't a worker before they'd even disappeared into the back room. Several women never appeared on the stage. Outside, Susan Cunningham was photographing the women as they entered, but Perry was making the connection as to whether they were there for work, or there for other business.

Perry smiled as another young woman walked up in front of him.

'Dance, soldier?' she said. Perry gave a smile, but it was false. He found the idea of handing over money for a sexual activity to be rather disappointing. If the woman had randomly pitched up and offered him such delights, he would have felt like the sexiest man in the world. For Perry, these places just didn't work, at least not as well as they should do.

'Not tonight, love,' he said. 'I've got to go. Maybe next time.'

The girl turned away, almost disgusted, and Perry finished his bottle of beer before leaving the premises. In truth, he was glad to be going. He was sporting a beard at the moment that was tickling. He also had a wig on that in the heat of the club caused sweat to run down into his eyes, stinging them. The interior was warm enough without any of these extras.

Perry exited the front of the club and saw Susan sitting in a car across the road. He then kept on walking to pick up a bus. She would pick him up six stops down and Perry sat, biding his time as the bus rolled on. Having been picked up by Susan, they made their way back to the hotel they were staying in and entered Perry's room. Susan sat down at the desk that had been provided in the room, while Perry collapsed onto the bed.

'Getting too much for you, is it?' said Susan.

'I don't get those places. You know that.'

'I'm sure you don't,' said Susan.

'There's no need to be sarcastic,' said Perry. 'I mean it.'

'You're telling me you've got a lot of young women jumping around, showing you everything, and you don't enjoy it?'

'It's not real,' said Perry. 'You know, it excites me, obviously. It's not a chore having to look at them, but there's no engagement. There's no—'

'Perry, you don't have to sell the story to me. It's okay. You can enjoy it. You're a man. I understand that.'

'No, you don't,' said Perry suddenly. 'You don't understand.'

'Oh,' she said.

'Well, you don't,' said Perry; 'sitting there saying, isn't it great to have this and to have that? It's not real. It's not what I want.'

'What do you want, Perry?' asked Susan suddenly and directly.

He realised he'd been cornered. This wasn't the conversation he wanted with Susan at the moment. As he sat there, he could also see Tanya's face. *What do I want?* thought Perry.

'More than that,' he said diplomatically. 'Let's get on with it.'

CHAPTER 08

Perry pulled his beard off, and took off the wig while Susan uploaded the photos from her camera onto her laptop. They spent the next half hour going through the photographs, for Perry to list where the women had gone. 'Dancer, not dancer, dancer, not dancer.' In the end, there were only four women who were not dancers.

'So, what have we got, surveillance-wise, from Glasgow? Has it been worth it?' asked Perry.

'Well,' said Susan, 'while you were enjoying yourself, they sent through some details. The teams down here have worked the clubs before, and they've got some photographs with names attached to it. Let's see if any of our four are found among their investigations.'

Perry disappeared for a shower while Susan ran the photographs that had come in from Glasgow and matched up the women that Perry had seen.

Perry stood in the shower, washing himself. He was trying to clear his head of thoughts of Susan and Tanya—two women he would like in his life in a fuller way, but also two that he wouldn't like together. Two that he didn't want to let down. Two that were, well, pursuing him—was that the word?

Perry didn't like complications in life, but this wasn't what was bothering him. He had sat there and seen the women enter the building, but he had the feeling some he had seen before. He was sure of it, but he couldn't say from where. Maybe it was faces of their parents he recognised, the likenesses. Maybe it was women in the past around Glasgow he'd seen. Perry was a mess in some ways, his mind racing, and that wasn't Perry. He was good at thinking, good at pulling out what was going on.

He stepped out of the shower, dried, and changed within his

own bathroom before stepping back out into the bedroom of the hotel. It was easier to work in one room rather than run back and forward between the two bedrooms Susan and he occupied. When he stepped back into his bedroom, he saw Susan's smile from behind the laptop sitting on the desk.

'Tell you what; let's call Emmett.'

Perry picked up his phone and told Emmett about the work they'd been doing and the fact they had potential links to four of the women.

'How long were you in the club for?' asked Emmett.

'We've been there the last couple of days.'

'Right,' said Emmett. 'There's a good chance we may have a link with these four women. It strikes me, though, where are all the men?'

'What do you mean?' asked Perry.

'When you get a group like this,' said Emmett, 'you'd expect it to be full of men, not lots of women.'

'But these women may not be in the group. These women may be just part of the normal underground lifestyle. I'm not saying they're not criminals, or that they may be part of the Revenge group.'

'It's possible. Let's take a look, pick our two best connections, and tail them.'

'How do we define which is our best?' asked Perry.

'Well, who's got things in common with the Revenge group?'

'Well, the club's owned by the McIntoshes. We're theorising that the McIntoshes could be in the middle of it. So, that sort of means everybody.'

'You've got to do better than that, Perry,' said Emmett. 'Come on, think. Was there anybody there who was looked after, cared for, did anything slightly different?'

'Let me think,' said Perry.

Perry tried to cast his mind back through the days. There were women who had gone in, but who had taken them in? How had they come into the club? He remembered some who entered and were almost straight out into the back office. Some had stayed, though. Then he remembered two who had come in separately, but one had been held in the club and then they'd gone through to the back.

'Hang on a minute, Emmett,' said Perry.

Perry turned to Susan and got her to put up some of the photographs from the Glasgow team. They had photographs of the McIntosh family as well, and he clicked through, before stopping on one.

'That guy there, is one of the McIntosh sons,' Perry said to Susan.

'What about him?'

'He was in the club.'

'Well, he runs it, or at least part of it. It's a McIntosh club.'

'Yes,' said Perry, 'but he was there. Hang on.'

Perry turned back to his phone, 'So Emmett,' he said, 'I've got two women who came into the club separately. Now remember, they were taken into the rear of the club by one person. A man came out and grabbed them, and brought them through.'

'And this is different because?'

'Some of the other women who came through and went to the back, they just went through on their own. These two, they were brought in, led through.'

'Have you got names for them?' asked Emmett.

'Hang on.' Perry started flicking through photographs on the laptop, photographs that were now linked to the photographs taken at the club by Susan. 'Jasmine Langer,' said Perry. 'According to the file, granddaughter of a McIntosh, partner, stooge, or something. The other one is Alice McGregor. And these two have gone in together. I think they're our best bet. I think that's where we start.'

'Sounds like a good idea,' said Emmett. 'I'll take one along with Sabine. You take the other with Susan. Keep a distance. Keep it at surveillance level only.'

'Will do,' said Perry.

'I'll be down with Sabine shortly. I think Glasgow is where we're going to end up working,' said Emmett. 'If the McIntoshes are involved we need to be all over it. With four of us there, it gives us more of an opportunity to look at things. In the meantime, send me up the details of this Jasmine Langer. I'll brief Sabine so we can get on to it as soon as we get down.'

Perry closed down the call and pointed at Alice McGregor. 'That's our girl,' he said to Susan. 'That's who we're tailing.'

'Emmett pulled the plug on the club, then.'

'Yes,' said Perry. He was glad. He'd done his work, but it had been a place of friction between Susan and him.

'Shall we go for some dinner?' asked Perry.

'Sounds good,' said Susan.

She closed down the laptop and went to leave along with Perry. But Perry suddenly stopped, pulling out his phone. 'It's a call,' he said. He looked at the phone. It was Tanya.

'Anybody important?' asked Susan.

Perry wondered what he should say. If he told Susan that Tanya was important, she might take that the wrong way. Or would she take it the right way? What was the right way? They were both important to him, after all, Susan and Tanya. The fact they were trying to manoeuvre past each other to get to him was, frankly, uncomfortable.

'It won't be a long call. It's just somebody I need to talk to, an old friend.'

'Okay,' said Susan. 'I'll get a table. See you down at the restaurant in fifteen minutes, yes?'

'Will do,' said Perry.

The door of the bedroom closed, and Perry picked up the call. 'Tanya,' he said. 'Why are you calling?'

'Just wanted to see you were okay. You been doing anything important?'

Perry paused for a moment. How did he answer this? This was a woman deeply interested in him, keen to take things to a romantic level. He was going to have to turn around and tell her he'd been surveilling a strip joint for the last couple of days.

'Can't talk about the case,' said Perry. 'Sorry, but not on this one.'

'But you are okay, aren't you?' she said.

'I'm fine,' said Perry. 'I'm doing okay. The shoulder and everything, it's healing. It's still sore, but I'm getting by.'

'Good,' said Tanya. 'Good. When you come back up, maybe we can talk, go for dinner.'

Perry could feel himself getting nervous now. He'd sat in a club with near-naked women all around him, offering him their wares, and he hadn't been nervous at all. He hadn't, in truth, been particularly excited. Now he had Tanya on the end of a phone a couple of hundred miles away, and he felt like a schoolboy, almost giddy with excitement. But he needed to think, and he just couldn't at the moment.

'Bit busy on the case at the moment. We'll see when I get back up. Maybe go for a coffee.'

'Just coffee?' said Tanya.

'Sorry,' said Perry, 'I just can't think. I'm tired.'

'Okay,' said Tanya. 'I'll go then.'

'Thanks for calling,' said Perry. 'I appreciate it.'

'Really?' said Tanya. And the call ended. Perry shook his head. Why did life get so complicated?

Chapter 09

Hope McGrath was sitting in the car with Kirsten Stewart beside her. They'd formed a good relationship when they'd started working together. That was before Kirsten had gone off to work for the Service, part of the UK's covert operations. Hope had been delighted when she'd seen Kirsten again, but the woman had changed from the young girl who had joined the team. She frightened Hope with how she could operate.

And yet, Kirsten was still there, at times bubbly, and always determined. One thing that Hope had loved about her was she had a mind like Macleod's, something that Hope envied. Hope wasn't that type of person, but Kirsten was, and at least she hadn't lost that while she was becoming a trained killer.

'Does it bother you sitting like this?' said Kirsten.

'Got to shift every so often. It doesn't feel great just to be sitting. But it's okay.'

'Always wondered about kids. I was going to have kids with . . . well . . .'

'Well, what?' asked Hope.

'There was someone when I was working with the Service. I thought we . . . well, I thought we could make it in that way.

We left the Service together.'

'What happened?' asked Hope.

'Well, it all went wrong,' said Kirsten. 'He got injured badly. He changed. And he's gone now.'

Hope studied Kirsten. 'That's not the entire story,' she said.

'I can't tell you the complete story,' said Kirsten.

'Can't or won't?'

'Both,' said Kirsten. 'Trust me, you're fortunate with John. You're best having somebody that holds down a normal job. A boring, normal job,' said Kirsten.

'I'll have you know that hire-car management around Inverness is quite exciting,' said Hope. 'Some evenings, he even comes home and tells me about the new stock they've got in.'

'He doesn't, does he?' said Kirsten.

'No, he doesn't. In fact, we don't talk about the hire cars that much. Talk about the people in it.'

'Are they interesting?'

'Not overly,' said Hope. 'But anyway, you see—'

'There!' said Kirsten suddenly. 'Bairstow! That's Bairstow!'

Hope glanced out of the car. Bairstow was indeed getting out of a car in front of Donato's and entering.

'Maybe you should—'

Hope stopped talking, realising that Kirsten had already left the car and was halfway across the road. And yet, she was moving in such a fashion that she didn't stand out, just looking like someone who was in a bit of a hurry to get somewhere. Kirsten disappeared inside Donato's, and Hope wondered what to do. She sat back.

Macleod had said to her to be surveillance only, and now she had Kirsten with her. At least she had an arm, if something needed looked at. Not that she'd told Kirsten to go in. Kirsten had just got up and gone. Maybe that was the Service in her. Maybe that was what they did. Much more on their own initiative. Hope would have to watch that.

Some more cars pulled up in front of Donato's, and several men got out, and a woman too. They seemed to look at each other, but the people with them seemed to look around the street. Some of the men went inside along with the woman, and some remained out on the street for a moment and then drove away in the cars. *Conspicuous*, Hope thought, *especially if you're being watched.*

She was debating whether to call Kirsten and tell her, but she would have seen who had walked in. Glancing along the road, Hope realised she wasn't the only person watching. She could see Ross, Patterson, and Clarissa had arrived in another car. They were chatting animatedly with each other, eyes focused on Donato's.

Hope watched carefully as Clarissa was clearly issuing instructions. Ross and Patterson stepped out of the car and made their way to Donato's. Once they'd gone inside, Clarissa climbed out, too. *Where is she going?* thought Hope.

The other two had gone inside. Hope decided to keep an eye on what was happening. She would float like a helicopter. That's what Macleod would want. Her watching, not getting too close, just in case things went wrong.

Clarissa, though, had disappeared from sight. *She hasn't gone into Donato's. So where has she gone?* Hope felt uneasy.

* * *

Kirsten had entered Donato's and gone over to look at the menu. She told the maître d' who appeared that she was thinking about a group coming here on another day and she wanted to check what sort of food was available. He left her in the corner, surveying the menu, as Ross and Patterson had arrived.

They had taken up a table, but the people who had come in ahead of them had gone straight through a back door into the rear. Kirsten was determined to get in there. You didn't have places in the rear without them being for a specific reason. Looking around the restaurant, this looked like a generous restaurant, plenty of space for many covers. Why would you have a separate place?

And the people that had arrived? Well, they gave off an air of knowing each other, but not as friends, more like business colleagues. While the maître d' was sorting out Ross and Patterson, Kirsten put down the menu. She floated towards the back door, and with no one looking, snuck inside of it.

There was a small corridor out to another room. It looked like a large room at the back, but there were toilets at the side of the corridor. Kirsten made her way into the toilets, locked herself in a cubicle, and put her ear up to the wall. She could hear voices inside, though the conversation was stilted.

Bairstow was clearly issuing instructions. Something about going elsewhere. He was waiting for others, apparently. And they would be going to a location. Although he didn't give that location out just yet. Were the others travelling with him? Kirsten wasn't sure.

One asked when they would get picked up. Bairstow made the point they would go through the door behind them into the alleyway for the cars that would come. It wouldn't take long. And when they did, they would then be whisked away to their meeting.

CHAPTER 09

Kirsten froze in her cubicle as someone entered the toilets. She didn't flinch, feet pulled up so anyone looking underneath wouldn't see her. She knew the door was locked to her cubicle, and if it was tried, this may show someone hiding there as opposed to being on the toilet. It was getting complex. If she needed to get out, she'd have to subdue people on the way, and her presence would be noted. She hoped it didn't come to that, but these were the risks you had to take. At least Hope wasn't with her.

* * *

Hope McGrath was getting agitated. She tried texting Clarissa, but there was no answer. So, she tried to ring, but the call was closed down. Clarissa wouldn't realise that Hope was sitting outside, that Hope knew where she was. Presumably Clarissa was in a kind of stealth mode and not wanting to talk at the moment. She'd be unaware, though, that Kirsten was inside.

It was important, though. The teams needed to connect. Kirsten would now know that Patterson and Ross were there, but she wouldn't know what they were doing, wouldn't know that Clarissa was in the vicinity. That could complicate things. Hope thought about Kirsten, the way she operated on her own. If she didn't know this variable, then things could go south. Could Kirsten deal with it without knowing all the factors? If ever there was a factor, it was Clarissa.

'Sod Macleod. Sod Seoras. I'm going to find out where Clarissa is. I'm going to find out. And then I'm going to get back in this car. Just so everybody knows what's going on,' said Hope to herself.

Having convinced herself, she stepped out of the car, wrapping her long coat around her, hiding her special bump, and she walked across the road. Clarissa had gone down the alley at the back, and so Hope followed her.

As Hope looked down the alley, she could see Clarissa just on the corner. She looked engaged in something, though. Hope wanted to whisper down to her, but she thought she might have to raise her voice too loud to be heard. So Hope crept slowly along the alleyway. She was only ten metres away when Clarissa turned around the corner ahead of her.

It was quite something to see somebody creep along in a tartan shawl and trousers, but then again, it was quite a shock to the system to see Clarissa tailing in a car. Clarissa wasn't the greatest at being covert, being subtle. Subtlety was not in her vocabulary.

Hope picked her pace up and got to the corner. She stole a glance into the alley beyond. The rear of the restaurant clearly came out here, and Clarissa was approaching a car. She was crouched down behind some bins, and a man was getting out of the car.

He looked left and right and then quickly rapped on the back door of the restaurant, but it was not a simple rap. It was a timed knock, two quick ones, then one after a pause, then another two quick ones, and after a pause, it was followed by three slow ones. The door opened, and he raced inside.

Hope wanted to call to Clarissa at this point, but the woman had moved out from behind the bins. She was looking into the car, and then she popped the boot open. It flew up. Hope could see her looking inside. Clarissa was heavily exposed. Hope could see that Clarissa was picking up some items and then she went round to the side of the car and looked into the mirror, scanning through the windows. She was shaking her head, muttering about something to herself, so much so she didn't see Hope frantically trying to wave at her. Even Hope's hushed calls went unnoticed.

Clarissa moved round to the back of the car when she heard something at the door. Hope had heard it too, and she wondered if Clarissa would get behind the bins. Her colleague looked panicked. But then she clambered into the boot and quickly pulled it down on top of her.

Hope could feel the sweat dripping down across her face. What was Clarissa doing? She could have just taken the number plate. She could have tailed. After all, that's what Kirsten and Hope were doing. Kirsten was finding out what was going on, but Hope was there to pick up a tail if necessary. Clarissa had three people. Why had she sent the boys in? And then to do this. Surely, she could have staged it better.

Hope was going to run forward and open the boot, except the door of the restaurant opened. Bairstow stepped out, along with the driver and a couple of other people. Hope's mobile began to vibrate. She reached down and pulled it out. It was Kirsten. She killed the call, and then quickly texted, asking Kirsten what she wanted.

The message came back: 'Bairstow on the move. Get car to tail. In alley at rear.'

'Clarissa in boot,' Hope texted back.

'What?' came the response.

'Clarissa in boot of car at rear. I am in the alley nearby.'

Hope had to fling herself back to the wall and crouch down as a car drove along the entry behind the restaurant and pulled up behind the other one. Two cars were suddenly being filled with people. Hope got herself back up on her feet and looked round the corner to see both cars pull away.

She started making a note of the number plates as her phone vibrated again.

'They're on the move!' it said. 'Follow!'

Hope turned, running back to the car. She jumped in, started it, and then the passenger door was suddenly open. Kirsten jumped in beside her, and Hope pulled out, cut across the traffic, trying to work out where the entry behind the restaurant would take the car.

'If this is him on the move, it might be to meet. It's important we stay with him.'

'Never mind that,' said Hope. 'Clarissa's in the boot.'

'In the boot?' blurted Kirsten. 'You meant she was actually in his car, in the boot. What the hell's she doing in the boot?'

'I think she was investigating. And then she got caught out and jumped into the boot.'

'How do you know?' asked Kirsten.

'Because I saw her go round. I wanted to know what she was doing. She didn't know you were on scene.'

'Bloody hell,' said Kirsten. 'Tail that car. Don't let it out of your sight. That woman.'

Chapter 10

'Stay on it. I can see it, but stay on it.'

Hope tried to remain calm as she drove along. Inside, she was shaking. Macleod had made it very clear the people they were up against were killers. They didn't hesitate. And now, Clarissa was inside one of their cars. If they were going to save Clarissa, they needed to stay with the car to know where Clarissa was. There was no guarantee, after all, that they could track her through a phone trace. There were two cars, however, ahead, for they'd both left the entry at the same time.

'And Clarissa's one is?' asked Kirsten.

'It's the one in the front. Do not lose the one in the front,' said Hope.

'I've got it,' said Kirsten. 'Just keep going. You're doing well. You're doing good.' Beside Hope, she could see Kirsten taking out a gun and checking it before putting it back inside her jacket.

'Is that going to be necessary?' asked Hope.

'Maybe not,' said Kirsten. 'But we're talking about the safety of an officer now. This is not about finding out information. This is about getting her back. Stupid woman,' said Kirsten.

'The cars are breaking up here,' said Hope.

'Follow Clarissa's one,' said Kirsten, as if Hope needed told.

'Of course,' said Hope. 'You'd better tell Macleod.'

'No, I'd better watch what's going on. Two pairs of eyes on it. You're okay, we're good, allright, we are good.'

The car was driving through Inverness and staying close to it was difficult. No doubt it would soon pull away. Hope stayed about four cars back, as they drove through the city centre, round a roundabout, and out the other side. But they seemed to go round and round the city. Then they drove across one of the bridges of the River Ness.

Reaching the other side, the car turned into heavy traffic down a street. Hope watched as it moseyed its way through and then sped up. It went to turn off down a side road, but another car came across. There was an incident. The other car swerved and hit four other cars, while the car containing Clarissa continued unabated. Traffic came to an instant standstill. Hope was now stuck five cars back, and the road was completely blocked with people emerging from their cars and shouting at each other.

'Damn it, damn it, damn it,' said Hope. She pulled out her mobile phone and called into the station. She recited off the car number plate, asking for everyone to be alerted before then calling Macleod and advising him what had happened.

'Lost her. She's inside the boot of the car.'

'What?' said Macleod. 'Easy, easy. She's inside the boot of the car. What the hell is she doing inside the boot of a car?'

Hope was fighting back tears. Kirsten took the phone off her. 'If I may,' she said. 'Seoras, that stupid woman's gone and got herself stuck inside the car. She's been trying to tail them or whatever. Bairstow is in it. I think he's off to a meeting.

CHAPTER 10

If she's inside the boot and they open it and she's there, she could be dead. We need to move on this. Get it out amongst all the police cars. Put it out, put it out wherever you can.'

'Have you tried phoning her?' asked Macleod.

'That's a risk. Her phone goes off and they hear it. She might be okay if she's in the boot and they stop and they all clear off somewhere and she can get out. We phone now, we put her at risk.'

'Text her,' said Macleod.

Kirsten picked out her own phone and texted Clarissa. She messaged: 'We know you're in the car. We know you're being driven around Inverness. We have been in pursuit, but we have lost you. Are you safe?'

A message came back. It was a jumble of misspelt words, but the consensus was yes. Clearly, typing inside the boot of a car wasn't easy.

'Do you know where you are?' messaged Kirsten.

'No.'

'Stay quiet. When the car stops, stay low and if you get a chance after that and there's no sound of anyone, see if you can open the boot to get out. You may be able to go in from the boot to the rear seats and out that way.'

Meanwhile, Macleod was on the phone to get Clarissa's phone tracked. If they could do it, it would help. Kirsten kept messaging Clarissa, maintaining the contact, and then Macleod was told that the phone was being tracked. They were now at a location just on the edge of Inverness. The car was on the move; it was still within the range of several mobile masts, but five minutes later, those tracing the phone advised it had disappeared.

'What do you mean it's gone?' said Kirsten. 'It shouldn't be gone. Either they stopped or—'

'Or somebody in the system has clocked we're doing it. These people are everywhere, Kirsten. They may have, well, they may have picked it up. Maybe they've gone into the back of the car. Is she still messaging you?'

'No,' said Kirsten.

'Right,' said Macleod. 'I'll take it from here.'

* * *

Tanya gingerly knocked on the door before getting a gruff 'Come in' from Macleod. She placed a cup of coffee down on the desk and then was silently retreating when Macleod turned round.

'Thank you,' he said. 'Um, no luck so far, before you ask.'

Tanya nodded and left the room. Macleod was pacing up and down behind his desk. He then picked up the coffee, drank some of it, and then marched downstairs. Hope had returned to the station with Kirsten. Ross and Patterson were back, too. They were gathered inside Hope's office, trying to work out what the next move should be.

'How are we doing?' asked Macleod, marching into the room without asking.

'It's not easy,' said Kirsten. 'We're getting the last known position of the phone. I will get out and start doing some searching. Patterson's going to come with me. We'll keep Hope here with Ross.'

'They're not likely to be there, though, are they?' said Macleod.

'By the looks of it, from what I can tell, the phone's been taken out of action. That probably means someone got hold of

CHAPTER 10

the idea we were tracing it, knew about it, called them, stopped them, and then, well—'

'Could she be dead, then?' asked Macleod.

'That's not a helpful comment, and we're assuming she's alive until we find her,' said Kirsten. 'I know everybody's very emotional at the moment. I know this is not looking good, but get your heads in it.'

'Of course,' said Macleod. 'I've got everyone from uniform onto it as well,' he said. 'She's well known; she's well liked. They'll all be pulling for her.'

'Good,' said Kirsten. 'I'll get out there.' As she went to go, Macleod stopped her.

'Maybe we get Pats and Ross out to the estate. See if we can work out where Bairstow is from his people.'

'We can try,' said Kirsten. 'I doubt they even know, most of them. And any inner circle he will know will be clued up enough not to give it out.'

'Still worth a punt, though, isn't it?'

'Yes,' said Kirsten. Macleod turned and looked at Patterson.

'Eric, change of plan. Get out in the car to the Bairstow estate. See if there's any clue as to where he is from his people. Ross, you stay here. You can handle this technology stuff. You know what you're doing with it.'

'And I'm on the move,' said Kirsten.

She went to leave, but Macleod grabbed her arm. 'Find her,' he said.

'I will do my darn best,' said Kirsten. 'Can I give you an instruction?'

Macleod looked at her. 'An instruction?' he said.

'Yes, you need to be doing something. At the moment, you're wandering around, not knowing what to do because you're not in her position.' Kirsten pointed over to Hope. 'So, go find out where this leak came from. How can we call up for a trace and then, within minutes, they know that we're tracking her, looking for the phone signal. They didn't even know she's in there. Because if they did, they'd have stopped a lot earlier and done it before. There are leaks in this place. There are leaks in this system, this force. Get on to that.'

Kirsten turned and stormed out the door. Macleod turned and looked at Hope. 'Are you okay?' he said. Hope's eyes were red, matching the colour of her hair, but not in a good way.

'Of course I'm not, but I've got a job to do, and she's just given you one. Get on it, Seoras.'

'If you need any help with that, sir,' said Ross, 'I can assist you.'

'Give me a contact for that office, for the people who were tracing it.'

Ross typed away into his computer, then handed over a number.

'Use your phone?' Macleod said to Hope, who simply nodded, and then swung over to sit beside Ross. Macleod took the phone.

'It's Detective Chief Inspector Macleod. I want to know who was tracing the phone of Detective Inspector Clarissa Urquhart.'

'Yes, sir, I'll just put him on for you.'

'This is Eric Pinkerton. To whom am I speaking?'

'You're speaking to Detective Chief Inspector Seoras Macleod, and you're going to give me some answers, son, and you're going to give me them fast.'

'You don't take that tone with me.'

'One of my officers is in peril. Deep peril because of your

CHAPTER 10

office and the fact that you can't keep a lid on what you're doing. Right. Who knew you were tracing this call? Who knew you were onto that phone?'

'Me? Just about everybody in the office.'

'You will write down—and the rest of your colleagues—what time you were in that room, and anytime you left. If you went for a pee, if you went for a sandwich, when you stepped outside. You will find out in that office who knew what was going on and who possibly could have stepped out to pass it anywhere else. You will have your phones all checked.'

'I think you'll find that we're a professional outfit here. There's no need for that sort of—'

'Ross,' said Macleod, his hand over the phone. 'Where's that place located?'

Ross passed the message, and Macleod thought of the location. England. England. That part of England. Who did he know? Who did he know? He turned back to the phone.

'Right. You're about to get a visit from a Detective Inspector John Malcolms. You will pay him every courtesy and answer every question that he asks. And we had better get to the bottom of this.'

Macleod closed the call, and then rang an old friend. Having instructed DI John Malcolms on the situation, Macleod thanked him as Malcolms raced out the door to investigate. Macleod sat down in Hope's chair. He looked at the team working away. Hope and Ross at the table. It brought back memories. It brought back Clarissa being outside and then thundering into the office. Her usual effort, no knock at the door, just barging in and demanding his time.

'She'll be okay,' he said to himself. 'She'll be okay. She has to be okay.'

He took a deep breath and then he called Emmett. 'Emmett! How are you getting on?'

'Got a couple of leads at the moment, Seoras,' he said. 'I'm tailing one with Sabine. The other is being tailed by Perry and Susan. They're women who went to McIntosh's gentlemen's club, the strip bar. Except they weren't there to work. These two, in particular, were taken through by one of McIntosh's sons. I want to see if anything comes from it.'

'As of now, you'll have to push harder. Be prepared to take risks,' said Macleod. He detailed the circumstances around Clarissa's disappearance.

'Understood,' said Emmett. 'We'll get on to it and see what we can do.'

'Don't force it, though. You're on a side that's very different. They may know nothing, but they may know something about locations. They seem to have had intel in the past on the Forseti group. I'm not saying the Revenge group's our best chance to find Clarissa, but it could present opportunities. Be aware.'

'I understand,' said Emmett. 'But we'll weigh the risks and move appropriately.'

'Understood,' said Macleod.

'This is Clarissa. She's a tough old cookie. She'll be okay.'

'Thank you,' said Macleod and put the phone down. He sat back. She was the Rottweiler. She barged in. Perfect for policing. She was that old school charge and do it, but this was not a normal police investigation. This required much more savvy surveillance. This required not shaking things up. And she had just charged straight in.

Should he have given her the role? Had he put her in a position she wasn't geared up for? He turned and looked out the window. It was his old office view. Much better than the one he had now from his own office. One that he'd loved, and in giving up the office for Hope to move upstairs, it had been one of the things he'd regretted.

'Stupid woman,' he said under his breath, 'you stupid woman. We'd better get you back.'

Chapter 11

'She's not doing much,' said Sabine.

'It's your go,' said Emmett. Sabine looked down at the small tray sitting between the two seats in the car. She picked up the five dice and rolled them, calculated the number, and looked at her chart to see where they could match up.

'You're going to win again,' said Sabine.

'You are getting better though . . . and it is a game of chance.'

'How can it be a game of chance if you keep winning?' said Sabine. 'But I refer you back to my earlier statement. She's not doing much.'

'She is the granddaughter of one of McIntosh's people, a man who was culled. Jasmine fits the bill. Most of the people in this Revenge group seem to have had some sort of background with the McIntoshes, and this culling. Either that or it was other people who were involved on the periphery. Matthews. People like that. So, she's a good bet. And Perry and Susan might get other ideas from Alice McGregor.'

'I bet you they're not playing dice games while they're watching.'

'It's only because they haven't been introduced to the wonder of it,' said Emmett. Sabine gave him a grin. But he was deadly

CHAPTER 11

serious.

'What I don't get—'

'There isn't anything else we can do, stuck here in a part of Glasgow, waiting, just waiting, and just—'

'You will not have to wait much longer,' said Emmett. 'Pack the dice up. There, she's coming.'

They watched as Jasmine Langer exited her flat and got into her small brown car. The girl was of an average height and build, but had purple flecks in her hair, which was mainly black. She wore leggings of a popular modern type, tight, along with a baggy jumper over the top. Sabine switched on the car engine.

After Jasmine drove past, she followed her and was soon able to pick up the gist of where she was heading. Shortly, Jasmine parked just along from the McIntosh's gentleman's club and made her way inside.

'Do we need to follow?' asked Sabine.

'No,' said Emmett. 'Just see how long she stays. We know she's not there to work. And it's hardly likely we're going to get in beside her and find out what's being said. Risky to blow our cover for that. So, we'll wait.'

Five minutes later, Jasmine Langer emerged, looking rather grim-faced. She jumped into her little brown car and drove off, causing Sabine to tail her again. This time, she headed outside of Glasgow, on the M80, and then out further towards the Campsie Hills.

Sabine was having to drive a little further back now, as the traffic thinned out. Eventually, Jasmine pulled over in a small car park that led to a forest. Sabine stopped a little beyond the car park, and together with Emmett, they sneaked back until they could see the car park and Jasmine standing with a man. Sabine took her camera, snapped a few shots, and then stood watching.

The couple seemed to be chatting, quietly at first, and then, almost without warning, they embraced passionately. Hands were roaming up and down backs and around buttocks, and right there in the car park they were kissing deeply. In fairness, the car park was empty. It still seemed a rather demonstrative effort, and Sabine wouldn't have been comfortable doing the same sort of thing with Emmett. She stopped herself.

Why did Emmett come into that conversation suddenly? Emmett wouldn't have grabbed her passionately like that. That wasn't Emmett. Why was Emmett being mentioned? Sabine knew why. But despite this she continued to watch, Emmett standing beside her, almost emotionless, looking at the lovers.

'How long do you think they're going to stay there?' asked Emmett.

'Well, they're clearly enjoying it,' said Sabine.

'Yes, but a car park. It's not very classy, is it?'

'Maybe they don't want to be seen.'

'Hang on a minute,' said Emmett. 'This isn't just some sort of random meet. She's gone to the strip club, and from it, immediately raced up here to the Campsie Hills. She wasn't going anywhere for ages. And what, oh, I'll just pop into the strip club on the way past to do this. I think she's gone there and got instructions to meet with this guy.'

'Who is he?' asked Sabine.

'I don't know. I don't know, but we'll find out. Okay. Get the photos off, see if anybody down in Glasgow station knows them.'

'Hey, up,' said Sabine suddenly. 'They're on the move.'

'Back to the car. Let's see where they go.'

Sabine and Emmett sat in the car and waited before the

CHAPTER 11

brown car went past them. Tailing at a distance, they didn't have long to wait before it turned off down a side road and ended up beside a farmhouse.

There were fields around it and plenty of cover with trees and walls. Sabine and Emmett parked up, expecting it to be for the night, as they saw the lovers go inside.

'It's quite big, isn't it?' said Sabine at the farmhouse. 'Good-sized shed beside it. Good base away from things, probably.'

'Possibly.'

'Do we get close?'

'No,' said Emmett. 'Not yet. We know things are on the move, so I'd rather watch.'

'But Clarissa's out there in trouble.'

'Maybe,' said Emmett. 'Maybe she's dead already.'

'You can't think like that,' said Sabine.

'I absolutely can think like that,' said Emmett. 'It's not palatable, but it's accurate. I don't want to see her dead, but if she is, the only way to get hold of these people and avenge her may be through this Revenge group. So, I don't want them to know we're watching.'

Sabine nodded, and the pair of them took turns through the night watching the house.

Emmett also sent the photographs taken of the man down to Glasgow, and was awoken at two in the morning, with a response saying that he was Scott Green, a notorious gunrunner. That piqued Emmett's interest. But it raised the question, why was Jasmine involved with him, and why was she linked to the strip club? Was this just a way the McIntoshes got their weapons?

It was around ten o'clock the next morning when Sabine woke. She had gone to sleep in front of the driver's wheel, but now she'd woken up having leaned to the side on Emmett's shoulder. She moved away with a start.

'Oh sorry,' she said.

'It's fine,' said Emmett. 'You looked tired. I thought I'd let you sleep.'

'I was meant to be on at nine. You're meant to get some sleep.'

'I don't need it. Besides, I think they're going to be on the move soon. Thought I'd let you get the rest so you could drive.'

'What makes you say that?' asked Sabine.

'They've been in and out of that shed several times this morning. I think they're packing stuff up. I think something's about to go on the move.'

'Really?'

'Just a thought,' said Emmett. The pair sat there and then watched as first Jasmine came out, followed by Scott. Together, the two stood in front of the cottage, kissing and holding on to each other, like they were at the end of some epic movie.

They then walked hand in hand over to the shed, opened it up, and revealed a van inside. Emmett and Sabine sunk low in the car. As the van pulled out of the shed, and after the shed was locked, the van departed back towards Glasgow. Sabine kept a respectful distance behind it, wondering if they would stop off at the forest, but it continued into the heart of Glasgow and eventually arrived at the gentleman's club.

It was driven round to the rear and entered through some gates. Sabine parked up and Emmett got out, walking closely over to the strip club. He tried to glance in through the back and saw that the van was being unloaded. However, its positioning was clearly to obscure anything from being seen entering the building. You would have to get up high and

CHAPTER 11

look down to have any sort of chance, but that would mean being up on the club roof and that wasn't going to happen. So, Emmett returned to sit in the car.

'What's going on?' asked Sabine.

'They're unloading things. He's a notorious gun runner, so it could be guns going in.'

'Get a raid going, then. Grab them while they're doing it.'

'Could do,' said Emmett. 'That's not what we want. We're looking to go beyond with this. We're looking to see where the whole Revenge group's coming from. At the moment, we're not sure if this isn't just some sort of McIntosh thing.'

'Got the feeling this is one and the same thing, though,' said Sabine.

'I'm not so sure,' said Emmett. He picked up his phone and placed a call, which was picked up by Perry.

'Morning, Perry. What's going on?'

'Still watching Alice McGregor,' said Perry. 'She's done nothing over these last couple of days.'

'Well, we can't all go to interesting places.'

'No,' said Perry. 'She's done nothing. She's just stayed in the house. I'm wondering if she's waiting for something.'

'What makes you say that?'

'She's not exactly an old person. A girl in her twenties will, at some point, make her way somewhere. They don't stay in all the time.'

'Different generation, Perry,' said Emmett. 'They may have got everything they want. Games, screens. They can live off their phones.'

'She came back from the strip club a few days ago, and she stayed put. I think she's waiting for something. She hasn't even been out for groceries; she hasn't had takeaway. Nothing,' said Perry. 'Something is up.'

'Well, I'm sitting outside the club at the moment, and currently, Scott Green, who's a gun runner, has driven a van down to it. Along with our Jasmine, they're offloading something into the club. I can't see what it is, but I would be surprised if it wasn't guns.'

'That's interesting. What would they want the guns for, though?'

'Well, I don't know. Might just be a McIntosh thing. Anyway, we'll stay and watch. You do the same. Let me know if anything's happened.'

Emmett continued to sit with Sabine until it got to lunchtime, and he ran out to pick up a couple of sausage rolls. As they sat eating them, Sabine found herself staring at Emmett.

'What?' said Emmett.

'Nothing,' said Sabine.

'You're staring over.'

'Girl can stare, can't she?'

Emmett gave her a quizzical look.

'What makes a girl fall for a guy like that?' said Sabine suddenly.

'Excuse me?' asked Emmett.

'I'm asking, what makes a girl fall for a guy like that?'

'And I have the answer because of what?' asked Emmett.

'Wrong way round really, isn't it? Guess I should be telling you why the girl's falling for him. Should I?'

'I don't get all this romance and falling in love and stuff. My problem is,' said Emmett, 'it's hard to find somebody who you get on with and who's into the sort of things you're into. I mean, I can't imagine being with someone who didn't enjoy the board games.'

Sabine smiled. She enjoyed the board games with Emmett and here she was right beside him and he wasn't saying anything. She thought maybe she should be more obvious. Maybe she could dress more provocatively. But she wasn't sure he would even spot it. That's not why he liked her. He barely even commented on how she dressed at all.

Not that Macleod or any of the others ever did, but that was different. That was because they were afraid that they'd say the wrong thing. Emmett never had that fear around her. He might say he liked her T-shirt, but he was usually talking about the motif, not her inside of it. She sat back. Maybe he wasn't the right one. Maybe this was just over-familiarity from working with him.

'Heads up,' said Emmett. 'On the move.' The gates at the back of the gentleman's club were pulled aside, and the van drove out, but there was only one person inside it. Scott Green was driving away.

'Do we follow?' asked Sabine.

'No,' said Emmett. 'Jasmine is our target. Jasmine's the one to follow. If they've dumped a load of stuff off, Scott is disappearing in the van. He's a gun runner, so that's pretty normal. We know his hideout now, anyway. So, I think the best thing to do is to stay put.'

There was a phone call. It was Perry.

'Emmett,' said Perry. 'We're on the move. She just got up all of a sudden, came out of the house. But she's heading downtown, and I think she's heading for the strip club. It's exactly the route that she would normally take to it.'

'Well, we're here already,' said Emmett.

'Jasmine inside?'

'Scott Green has now driven off in the van. He's left Jasmine inside, and now Alice McGregor's coming too. I wonder if there's going to be any others.'

'Sounds ominous,' said Perry. 'Possibility of guns being added into the mix?'

'I know,' said Emmett. 'It does look that way. Keep your eyes on her.'

Chapter 12

Clarissa woke with a jolt, and then she felt the pain. It was like her shoulders were separating. Her eyes cast a glance up above her, and she saw a large hook with some leather ties which were wrapped around her wrists.

Dangling from the hook, her shoulders were driven upwards, her feet shy of the floor. She was aware of a sudden chill within the room and realised that she was simply in her underwear. Thankfully, it was practical underwear. It was large, covered plenty, and not the items she'd worn during Frank's birthday. In truth, it was of little comfort.

She tried to work past the pain she was feeling from her shoulders. It was dull, not so intense, but constant. She didn't think anywhere else was hurting. At least it wasn't hurting as bad.

Clarissa tried to look around the room. It was dark, with a blind across a window. She knew it must have been a window, because the side of the blind had light coming past it, almost like the edges of an angel. She tried to twist her head around. Clarissa could only see shadows, her eyes slowly becoming accustomed to what was out there. There was a man. There was definitely a man there.

She watched as he stood up and came over to her. He must have been at least forty and had a grizzled face. He came up close to her, his hand running across her belly.

'I like the old girls. Bit more to them. Understand what a guy wants, too. Young'uns have no idea, do they? Unlike you. You feisty number, you.'

Clarissa spat in his face, and the man swiped the back of his hand across her chin, sending her spinning.

'You can cut that out,' said the man, wiping his face. 'You're lucky. I could have taken it all off of you. So just be a good girl.'

Despite being hung up, despite the obvious pain in her shoulders, and the threat of being left completely starkers in front of this man, Clarissa was most upset by his use of the term 'girl.' She'd been called many things in her life, but at this point, 'girl' was no longer a compliment. It was a derogatory remark that spoke of Clarissa being useless. A good girl. She could have handled the term 'filly.' She could have handled the term 'bitch.' But she did not like being referred to as a good girl. If she got down, that man was getting it full bore.

'You're trying to look tough there, aren't you?' said the man. 'Once we get what we want out of you, you'll be fish food. Although we may have to drive a bit to find the fish. Oh, is that a clue? Don't worry, they won't be looking for you. I doubt they want to come for you, anyway. You were daft enough to get into the boot of a car. I mean, what a show. Couldn't have worked out better for us.'

The man stepped forward and gently spun Clarissa. Her ties went round and round the hook they were hanging on, and she wondered what he was doing, until when she had turned fully away from him, he planted a large smack on her backside.

CHAPTER 12

No doubt it left a large red mark.

'That's the girl. That's better. Suppose you're not bad for sixty-five,' he said.

Sixty-five! raged Clarissa inside. *Sixty-five!* She was ready to kill him. And then the door opened. She saw little as someone pulled the blind, and Clarissa blinked at the sudden sunlight, forcing her to squint.

'Well, well, well,' said a voice. 'I'd like to say it's good to see you, and I mean that. You're an ignorant one, aren't you? And jumping in my boot. How kind of you. Well, you're away from all your followers now. You've got nobody to look after you out here. Thing is, I think we'll have fun with you here for a bit. And then, well, we'll finally get to your Frank as well. I don't know who saved him last time.'

Clarissa grimaced, but she had no idea what the man was on about.

'Cost a fortune, that guy, too. You must have some friends. Not enough, evidently. Not enough to stop you being a stupid arse.'

Clarissa was still spinning, and Bairstow regarded her. 'Well, I've seen worse,' he said, and gave her a huge smack on the backside as she spun past, causing her to spin even more. 'I'd love to stay and chat. Actually, I really would. I'm also wondering how many people I could get in here. Clarissa Urquhart, apparently the scourge of the arts world. I wonder what they'd pay to see you like this, to come along and have a bit of fun. I don't know. Still, I've got business with the king, first. Then I'll be back to deal with you.'

'I'm wondering about leaving you alone,' said Bairstow, 'but then again, you're not going anywhere, are you? Are the shoulders sore yet?' Clarissa grimaced.

Bairstow turned, whispered something to the man in the room, and then the pair left, Clarissa still swinging round in a very slow motion. For a moment, she almost felt sorry for herself. She wondered what she'd done to be in this position. But then, self-preservation kicked in, and she looked up and around at what was binding her. It was a simple hook up above, but they'd cleverly done the ties around her wrists, so she couldn't get her hands close enough together to undo them. Instead, she just swung.

What she needed to do was to lift the strap that kept her hands tied together, off from the hook from which she hung. If she could get her feet on the ground, it wouldn't be that difficult. Indeed, any sort of purchase. But right now, she was struggling to see anything, and she wondered if she would tire more and more as the day went on.

Clarissa's eyes were slowly becoming more accustomed to the light, and then she saw a chair that was beside where Bairstow had been. Had he been sitting on it. Who knew? Frankly, who cared? Clarissa tried to swing.

She knew she'd done this when she was young. Move slowly back and forward like the ever-increasing pendulum. And then maybe, just maybe, she could reach the chair with her feet.

That's what she wanted, after all. If she could get her feet to that chair, she might drag it over. And if she could get her feet firmly planted, she could get off the hook. It was worth it. Worth a shot, because after all, what did her future look like at the moment? Would they come back and sexually harass her? Would they cut her? Bleed her? Would they punch and kick her? Torture her?

Or would they simply just end it? Walk in and put a bullet in

CHAPTER 12

her head. She'd try not to think about these things. But then, Frank's image came up in her mind. She couldn't leave him like this. Would they go for him, too?

She swung harder, reached out with her feet, and her big toe touched the top of the chair. The chair rocked, but it didn't move, and she continued to swing back and away from it.

She tried another three times, the pain in her shoulders increasing, and when she missed it the third time, she cried. She hung there, tears falling off her cheeks, until she decided it was time, time to do more. Once again, she swung for the chair.

Come on, old girl. Come on, you can do it. You've got this. She swung and swung again, reached out with her foot and kicked the chair so that it bounced and turned over. It fell so far away from her she couldn't get near it. Clarissa did everything she could to stop the flow of tears.

How did she manage that? How was she so useless at this age? In her day she'd have caught that no problem. In her day, she'd have handled these guys and given them a right thrashing. Would anyone be coming for her? Would Macleod have the search on the go? Did anybody know where she was? They must have done; they had texted. But even then, how can you text back when you're bouncing about inside a car?

Stop it, Rissa. This was her name. Deep inside. At that moment, she talked to herself. Rissa. *Come on, Rissa.* Rissa was something inside that just wouldn't crack. Deep down, there for the darkest of times. And this was dark, almost hopeless. She was an Urquhart. Proud of the family name. Proud of what they did. Proud of her antiques heritage. She could do this. And then Frank's face appeared again before her. No, she'd do it for him.

Clarissa looked up at the big hook that the strap hung off that bound her hands. If she could swing, she might be able to get it off. She'd have to really swing, though. She'd have to get to that point where you were swinging so far you almost lost the pull on the bind. The bind would lift enough, and she'd throw her hands up and maybe she'd sail off the hook. But she'd have to swing. Well, she used to be able to swing.

She remembered swinging. When she was younger, in the gym, she could swing. Clarissa tried to let her body hang easy. And then she moved her ankles and hips, backwards and forwards, slowly building up a swinging motion. At each end of the swing, she could feel her shoulders feel like they were getting pulled out. But she encouraged herself.

She had to go quicker. She had to do more. Through gritted teeth, she swung back and forward, back and forward, until suddenly it was like the bind had moved. The bind above her had moved along the hook just a fraction. She kept swinging and she could feel it move again. It was getting closer to the edge of the hook now and she didn't want that because the hook curved back on itself.

She'd have to swing where she was and then lift the bind up quickly. In a heroic effort, she'd have to throw her arms up before it moved too far forward and was caught inside the partial circle of the hook.

Come on, Rissa. Come on!

And off she went. Clarissa didn't think. She just did. Now she could see her feet almost coming up level with her, but she could also feel her shoulders almost being ripped out from her back. Another couple, that's all she'd need, another couple.

She swung back and forward, flicking her feet, flicking the hips forward, driving until she felt that bind lift completely.

CHAPTER 12

She wasn't being supported by it anymore and with every effort, every ounce of strength she had, she flung her arms upwards. The bind cleared the hook and Clarissa flew forward and down, crashing hard onto the floor.

She stopped for a moment, breathing in. Was she all right? Had she made it? Slowly, she pulled herself up on her feet. She needed to get out of here. She needed—*no,* she thought, *I'm going to have them*—and she staggered around the room.

Her hands were still tied together, but that didn't mean she couldn't search. At least now she could bring them close together. She looked around the room she was in. It was practically bare, so she approached the door. For a moment, she wondered if it would be locked. She tried it. It wasn't. *Well, they made a mistake with that one, didn't they?*

She pitched out into another room. There was a large table. On the table were several bits of paper, beer cans, and empty takeaways. Clarissa pored over the paper. There was a map.

This is the Cairngorms, isn't it? thought Clarissa. She recognised some names. *This is the Cairngorms.* She looked again. There was a site on it denoted by a large X. *That's the middle of the Cairngorms. What's that about?*

She raced around, pulling open drawers and a few of the old furniture cupboards that were kicking about. Most were empty. Some contained more food or a sleeping bag. She went into the next room, found other maps, but these weren't marked. These had nothing on them but were parts of the Cairngorms. So, what was this about?

Clarissa searched another cupboard down at the bottom. Pulling out the drawer, she recognised her old faithful. She reached with her hands and grabbed her tartan shawl, holding it close to her face, tears streaming. This was hers. Then her mobile was maybe here, too. What did they do to it? She dug inside, and it was there. Her mobile. Her mobile was there. It was switched off, but it was there.

She thought back. They'd stopped the car, the boot had opened, and then it went black. Maybe they'd done something. Maybe they'd switched it off then. If she could switch it back on.

Clarissa pressed it, praying that there would still be power remaining. And when the screen lit up, she found herself having to wipe it clear as the tears hit it.

'Think. Think, Clarissa,' she said. 'What have we got here? What have we got in front of us?' She looked down at her call list. Macleod. She pressed it and waited. The other end of the line suddenly picked up.

'It's Seoras.'

'Seoras,' she said. And she wept again.

'Are you okay? Where are you?'

'I don't know,' said Clarissa, 'but I'm okay.'

Chapter 13

'Clarissa?'

'Seoras, is that you? Seoras, tell me I've got you!'

Macleod was standing in his office and had just picked up his mobile phone, which had vibrated. He'd seen the number, the legend on the screen, 'Clarissa Urquhart,' and had hoped against hope.

'Seoras, I'm stuck out somewhere in the country. I'm in a . . . like a farmhouse . . . somewhere.'

'Are you hurt?' asked Macleod.

'I'm okay. They hung me up. They've left me here because they've gone somewhere. Look, there's a location, a map. It's up into the Cairngorms.'

'You're in the Cairngorms?' asked Macleod.

'I don't know where I am. I haven't looked, but there's a map. There's a map and there's a site marked on it. Here.' Macleod could hear the phone being rotated. And then a message popped up a moment later, showing a map with an X on it, a site marked.

'Where's that?'

'Loch Lee. Loch Lee up in the Cairngorms. You need to get there,' said Clarissa. 'That's where they're off to, I think.

Anyway, they headed out. They headed out to meet the king.'

'The king?'

'I think it's the boss, the head honcho. I think this is what it's all about. Bairstow . . . Bairstow had me.'

'I know they took you from behind that restaurant.'

'I hid in the boot,' said Clarissa. There was silence. 'It was a really stupid idea,' she said.

'Yes, it was. Can you get away?'

'I can. Hang on, I'll put the map function on the phone again. I'll see if I can find where I am.'

Macleod stayed silent, understanding that Clarissa was working on her phone. However, he pressed the intercom, requesting Tanya's presence.

'Seoras, I'm on the edge of the Cairngorms. I'm not that far away. You need to come. You need to come get me before they get back. I'll move outside. I don't want to go too far. Maybe I can find a road, but . . .'

'Stay put, stay hidden,' said Macleod. 'By all means, go out of the building, but make sure you don't go too far. I'm on my way. Keep your phone with you. I'll message you once I understand everything else that's going on.'

There was a rap on the door, and Macleod told the knocker to come in.

'You called, Seoras?'

'Yes. Just made contact with Clarissa. Get me Hope. Get me Kirsten.'

'Of course,' said Tanya. But she gave Macleod a smile before she turned.

Macleod picked up his own phone and called Emmett.

'Emmett, just heard from Clarissa. We've got her. What's happening with your contacts?'

CHAPTER 13

'Both are still on the move. Apparently, both going towards the same point by the looks of it. We're tracing them separately but I've got the feeling we're coming together.'

'And what do you suspect is going on?'

'There seems to be a gathering in progress. I think there's a meeting here going on with the Revenge group, or something more. It's just, there was such a low level of activity, and then suddenly everyone seems to be on the go.'

Macleod informed Emmett about the site that was marked up by Loch Lee.

'Well, I can't say we're going there at the moment, but I'll keep an open mind on it. We are heading towards the Cairngorms. We're at the southern edge of it.'

'Well, stick to it. Advise me if anything else happens. I'm going to get Clarissa.'

Macleod closed down the call. There was a rap at the door, and it opened to reveal his red-headed detective inspector.

'Sorry to barge in. You got her?' said Hope.

'Got a location, and we need to go. Get some uniform backup,' said Macleod.

'You want Kirsten to come with us? She's working with me downstairs.'

'No,' said Macleod. He then looked beyond Hope to see Kirsten entering the room.

'What's happened?' asked Kirsten.

'She's called in. She's got herself free. Apparently she was held, hung up. Now she's free, and she's got her phone. I've told her to stay roughly close to where she is, but get out of the building.'

'I'll go get her,' said Kirsten.

'No,' said Macleod. 'I'll go get her with Hope. Listen. She

found some details. There's a spot marked close to Loch Lee in the Cairngorms. She believed her captors may be going there. They're off to meet the king, the head of the organisation, by the sounds of it,' said Macleod.

'You go there,' he said to Kirsten. 'You've got all the skills to watch, and if necessary, bring backup in.'

'You want me to bring backup in?'

'Your call. I'm saying you can do. You'll be able to judge the situation. You could be walking into a horde of people, or a small number. Who knows? Clarissa just said they were all going. They all left the house that they were holding her in. Not one of them left behind.'

'That's unusual. Not one of them. How did she sound?'

'She sounded okay. A bit distressed, but sounded like Clarissa. There was nothing to indicate she wasn't free to leave, clear to get away.'

'Loch Lee, I'm on it. But you get over to Clarissa quickly, though,' said Kirsten, 'and make sure you take people with you.'

'I'll get hold of Ross and Patterson,' said Hope.

'Good idea. Now we need to go,' said Macleod. He walked over, picked up his coat and his hat, and was about to leave when Tanya came back in.

'Just had the ACC on the line. He's asking what's going on. Have you heard anything?'

'Thank you, Tanya,' said Macleod. 'I'll speak to him on the way.'

He left, racing down the stairs as best he could, out into the car park. Hope flagged him over towards her car, and Macleod called the ACC.

'Jim,' he said, 'Clarissa's called in. She's managed to free herself. She's being held in the Cairngorms. I'm off to get her.

CHAPTER 13

However, there's also another meeting going on. Those who were holding her all left to meet who they described as the king, probably the head honcho of the organisation. It's at Loch Lee in the Cairngorms.'

'Have you got someone going there?' asked Jim.

'I've left Kirsten to keep an eye on that one. Could be a big event. We don't want to give anything away. If she feels we can grab them all, she'll call in.'

'Okay,' said Jim. 'Let me know when you have Clarissa.'

Macleod closed down the phone call as Hope reversed the car and headed off. His hands were sweaty, but his heart was lifted. *She's alive*, he thought. *She's actually alive.* He'd been preparing himself to find out she was dead. This was an unexpected twist, but it was a good one.

* * *

'Looks like they're pulling up, and it looks like they're pulling up to a party,' said Sabine.

She was driving Emmett as they tailed Jasmine Langer. Jasmine was currently pulling her car in beside a large farmhouse. There were some other outbuildings around it, but Sabine had to drive past and park up some distance away. As they got out of the car to look with their binoculars towards the farmhouse, they saw other cars pulling in, and some vans.

And then, a car sailed right past, before pulling up just beyond them. It was Perry and Susan.

'Alice McGregor's gone in there as well,' said Susan. 'Made straight for it.'

'We could only have been a couple of minutes ahead of you,' said Emmett. 'They're gathering. I don't like this, though.'

'Do you want to get closer?' asked Perry. Emmett thought for a moment.

'We need to be careful. That's a good number in there. We don't want to get caught. It will not be that safe.'

'I can get up close,' said Sabine. 'Won't bother me.'

'I'm sure it won't, but let's let them settle down for a moment. You don't want to be getting close when there's more people arriving. Let's just hold our horses. Do some surveillance from a distance. Get the camera out, Perry. See if we can get any photographs of them.'

It was about thirty minutes later when Emmett was getting the feeling that maybe Sabine could get closer. Several other cars and vans had arrived and there must have been a good fifteen or sixteen people in there.

'Get yourself ready,' said Emmett to Sabine. 'You'll move over in about five minutes. I want Perry and Susan to flank you so they can see you.'

'I'd hold that thought for a moment,' said Perry.

Emmett looked up. The farmhouse looked like it was bleeding people, so many were emerging from it, jumping into vans. They were wearing masks, although they were pulled up on top of their heads.

'Do you see any weapons there?'

'I think so,' said Perry.

'Right then,' said Emmett. 'Get the car ready. We're going to tail them. Perry, I want you and Susan to remain here. Keep an eye on that farmhouse. Anybody else comes and goes. Let me know what's going on.'

'Will do,' said Perry. Emmett got into the car and with Sabine they watched as the vans disappeared off further into the Cairngorms rather than back towards the A9.

CHAPTER 13

'Where do you think they're going?' asked Sabine.

'I don't know, but just hold back; keep them at a distance.'

'It might have been better to have Perry and Susan with us, two cars to keep an eye on them.'

'I don't want Perry anywhere near this. He's not fit for action yet. He's doing a good job, but they have guns.'

'You don't go away with guns in that number unless you're going to use them,' said Sabine.

Emmett told Sabine to keep a distance but keep following. They ended up deep into the Cairngorms, on a road that led up towards Loch Lee.

'This is where the boss was saying the other lot were going,' said Emmett.

'I think they might be pulling over, though,' said Sabine.

She continued along as the vans pulled off to one side. Sabine drove on further before stopping. The two of them quickly got out. The night was getting darker, and Emmett went to text Macleod to say where he was, but there was no signal.

'Damn it,' said Emmett to Sabine. 'We need to keep following them. Get the message back as soon as we can.'

"I could go on alone," said Sabine.

'No. Not with this lot. Two of us have got a better chance if somebody comes at us. We stick together.' They went into the boot of the car, pulled on black clothing, as well as pocketing some hand torches. Sabine had the camera tucked away inside her jacket.

'Stay close,' said Emmett. Together, the two turned to look for the vans. Although the night was dark, there was enough moonlight that Sabine could see shadows moving up ahead. She was better at tracking than Emmett ever was, so he let her go ahead of him, although he was only a few feet behind.

The ground was rough, and although there was a path, Sabine chose to not use it. Soon, they were rounding Loch Lee, heading off-path, and they came to a point where they could see torchlight in the distance.

'I wonder what that is?' Sabine whispered to Emmett.

'We need to get close,' he said. 'But keep us a distance behind them. I don't want to be right up close if shooting starts.'

'True,' said Sabine. 'I'll keep us a distance back.' She continued to follow, walking through the rough landscape of tough grass, and the blossoming heather.

As they got closer, Sabine saw those in front of her suddenly crouch down. They were fanning out, making a circle. The torchlight was clearer now—set up towards stones in a circle. She looked through the camera to get a better idea, letting the infrared do its work.

'Emmett,' she said softly, 'there's like a circle, a Forseti circle stone, one like Clarissa found. There are also people sitting on the stones. It's like there's a meeting in the middle. There's a stone but it's got empty cracks in it, but it's empty, there's nobody sitting in it. Hang on a minute,' she said and spun the camera on the different people sitting on the stones.

'They've got hoods up. I can't see most of them.' And then the camera focused on to one person. 'That's Bairstow,' she said, trying not to lift her voice. 'Bairstow, and he's holding a knife in his hand. It's like one of those ritual ones.'

'Can you hear him?'

They were still some distance away, but Emmett could hear Bairstow's voice in the breeze. Sabine continued to look around with the camera.

'They're forming a circle,' said Sabine. 'They're coming in, going to come in and envelop him. They're going to take him

CHAPTER 13

out, Emmett. Believe it or not, they're going to take all of them. They've got them. They've actually got them.'

Chapter 14

Kirsten Stewart was hunkered down in the grass, watching the rather strange ritual taking place in front of her. Several men, and possibly a few women, had arrived. They had hoods on, covering their faces, but one was exposed, and he had no problem with walking around with his face uncovered. This gave Kirsten a sense of apprehension.

Generally, you covered your face because you didn't want anyone else to know who you were. And especially in these sorts of rituals, brothers and sisters of a particular order didn't want to know who each other was. It was too easy to give things away then. Bairstow had the map, as Kirsten saw it, and had come here and yet seemed to lead the proceedings. Something wasn't sitting right with her.

The stone circle was not natural. These stones would be put here, because a stone circle like this would have been recorded on maps. It would have been noted. So, why would they come here? It wasn't making sense to Kirsten. Some things were just not tying up. And when things didn't tie up, Kirsten got nervous.

She also wasn't carrying a weapon at the moment, which was bothering her. She had come to do reconnaissance. That had

CHAPTER 14

been the plan, but with the feelings she was getting, and the uneasiness, she wondered if she should disappear and come back with a gun or possibly come back with a lot more people. Reconnaissance was easy when it was just yourself. Much harder with numerous people, especially those who didn't understand how to do it properly.

As she scanned the surrounding area, Kirsten knew that on the far side from which she sat, a large group of people was slowly approaching. She was far enough back from the scene that she could see them spread out. They appeared to be dressed in dark colours and some of them were carrying weapons. She held a small set of binoculars to her eyes and she got a shock when she saw beyond that group. Two more people sneaking forward. They weren't doing a poor job of it, but Kirsten could pick them out. It was Emmett and Sabine.

Kirsten watched as the group slowly spread out and encircled the stone circle. They were quite a distance from the centre, but some were starting to get close to her, having spread out to make the circle. But Kirsten was okay, hidden away and watching. Then she saw them enclose on the circle. Meanwhile, in the middle of the stone circle, Bairstow was still standing and ranting. Some of the words were definitely not English.

Kirsten took out her phone. Maybe she should try to call Emmett. They were far enough back, weren't they? She rang through and watched him as his hand went towards his phone. However, it seemed that the signal stopped. She looked down at the connection. It was intermittent at best.

Kirsten had come upon the circle, with most of the people already installed. Kirsten had been the last to join them. She now scanned the figures at the stones. Maybe they were being respectful, but they didn't move. There was no movement from them at all.

This made her think. Macleod had said that Bairstow had left behind the map. Clarissa had been tied up. How had she got free? Clarissa wouldn't have been hard to hold. But instead, Bairstow had left with everyone, leaving her alone in a house. She had been able to find her mobile phone and call Macleod. Some things didn't make sense. It was either incredibly amateur or was it something else?

Kirsten scanned the scene again. There were shapes that she didn't like. She wasn't sure, because it was hard from the distance she was at. Were more people moving out there? She squinted her eyes, rubbed them, and looked again.

Watching through binoculars could be difficult to pick people out. Sometimes perspective is a major factor on seeing things move. Too close, you can't see them. But when you're further back, and the shades come to you differently, sometimes you see things you wouldn't see right up. This is what was happening to Kirsten.

Kirsten tried to call Emmett again. He was not that far behind the enclosing Revenge group circle, but these shapes that were moving were beyond Emmett. Further out, the two of them were at the same time. But those shapes were moving in, in towards the stone circle.

Kirsten saw it clearly. In the middle was Bairstow and his group. Beyond that, a ring of the Revenge group. And beyond that, Emmett and Sabine. And yet beyond them, something moving in quickly.

No motion. No motion at the stones, she thought. She needed to call Emmett. But nothing was getting through quickly. She texted him, and it simply said, 'Emergency. Hit the ground

CHAPTER 14

now.' She pocketed her phone, put the binoculars inside, and began to run forward.

Bairstow was chanting now and coming to the middle of the circle. But the middle of the circle was where you sacrificed people. Where Clarissa pondered you might despatch wrongdoers. She expected that there might be some motion from those in the hoods, but again, there was nothing from them.

Kirsten was out with the line of shadows moving in. But now on the move, she saw one coming in close. Looking ahead, she saw Emmett and Sabine suddenly drop to the ground. Not a moment too soon, for behind them, and all around the circle of the Revenge group, figures in black leapt up from the ground, guns in hand.

What an absolute nightmare, thought Kirsten. But while she thought, she ran. There was a man in front of her, looking in and firing at the Revenge group in front of him. Gunfire should have been splitting the air but the quiet click of silenced weapons was the only audible betrayal of the killing until the bodies hit the ground. Kirsten came up behind him, arm around his neck, snapped it, and took his gun off him. From there, she ran towards the centre of the circle.

The Revenge group was getting cut down. They'd got so close to the stone circle but were now running here and there for their lives. Despite the gunfire, none of the figures sitting in the circle had moved, except for Bairstow, who was now reaching the inner stone. Even retaliatory gunfire from the revenge group, which was not silenced, failed to provoke a reaction. Some of the Revenge group were firing at Bairstow, but the men behind them were soon taking them down.

Kirsten turned and despatched one of the hidden men, before hitting the ground herself as gunfire sailed over her head. She didn't, however, stop crawling forward before getting up again, running to one side, and assessing where she was.

What were her options? What would Macleod want her to do? This was murder. This was the Revenge group being taken out. But Kirsten couldn't defend them. She was one person. And these guys with guns, they weren't idiots. They could use them.

Kirsten stole up behind another one of the men, reached into his side, took his gun out of his pocket and despatched him from behind with it. She then held him standing upright as bullets flew, trying to protect herself. From there, she ran quickly and got behind one of the stones that provided the seating to the people in hoods. The figure on the stone was hit and tumbled to one side. It did not, however, cry out. The hood fell away, and Kirsten saw the mannequin.

All a set-up. All one big set-up. The gunfire was more sporadic, now, more the quiet clicks of silenced weapons than the bare sound coming from the guns of the Revenge group. The initial round of fire must have taken out several of the Revenge group, but there were still some there, and occasional loud gunfire was still happening. In the darkness, it was difficult to see all that was going on, but in the middle of the circle, still lit up by torchlight, was Bairstow.

He was holding the knife up now. The gunfire from the Revenge group reverberated through the hills, but the men in black were shooting with accuracy and with purpose. Their gunfire was also silent, so the Revenge group couldn't tell where they were coming from.

Kirsten was holding her ground, hoping that Emmett and Sabine had held theirs, too. She looked up and saw Bairstow

CHAPTER 14

crying out to the night before he took the sacrificial knife up to his own throat and cut it. For a moment, the man stood, and then a gunshot sent him spinning. The knife fell from his hand, and he dropped to the floor.

Kirsten decided that meant it was time to go. There was nobody here to pump for information, not at the risk to get it. She'd get Emmett and Sabine and get out. Once again, she crawled forward, up behind a man in black who didn't see her coming. It was a moment to break his neck, another to then get on the move and take his gun with the silencer on the end. In the grass, she picked off two of the men in black, close to where Emmett and Sabine were. She worked quickly towards them.

Just stay put, she said to them in her mind. *Just stay put and I'll get you.*

But Emmett wasn't staying put. Emmett was now up out of the grass and running forward into the middle of the circle. She watched Sabine look at him with panicked eyes and then follow.

'Blast it,' said Kirsten, and was up out of the grass. There was a man in the circle possibly from the Revenge group, looking at Emmett, but as his gun was lifted, he had no chance to fire it. Kirsten despatched him. She ran hard as Emmett approached. First, though, Kirsten could see other guns being pointed, and she hit Emmett hard, knocking him to the ground. She heard the quiet bullets fire over the top of them. She hoped Sabine had got herself down.

As she looked around from her prone position, she could see Sabine. But Emmett was crawling in towards Bairstow.

'What's it all about?' asked an intent Emmett. 'Who were you here to see?'

'The king,' said Bairstow. 'All for my king. You'll never find him. You'll never find the king.'

Kirsten crawled up by Emmett. 'What are you doing?' she said. 'We need to get out of here.' Emmett was rifling through Bairstow's pockets and the long gown he had on.

'Leave him!'

'It's the end of the line. This is the end of the connection,' said Emmett. 'There has to be something in here. He can't just die here without giving us something else.'

'Don't you see? He's killed himself. He's killed himself to bring them in,' said Kirsten. 'He's taken out the Revenge group.'

Sabine crawled up beside her, and put her hand on Emmett's. 'And they'll take us out if we don't get out of here,' said Sabine. 'Listen to her.'

Kirsten got up into a crouch behind the stone, looked around, took down one man with a silenced gun, then another, and then crouched again.

'Over there,' she said, 'that's where there's the least of them. You two will run, I will cover you, and then I will follow.' She grabbed another gun lying on the ground beside a despatched body, and handed it to Sabine. 'You know how to use this?'

'Not really,' said Sabine. 'I can probably fire it.'

'Anyone gets in your way,' said Kirsten. 'Take them down, anyone. There are no friendlies here, just the three of us.'

Sabine nodded, and Kirsten popped her head up from behind the stone again. She fired twice, then turned back. 'Go!'

Sabine was up on her feet in no time, but Emmett was slower. As he ran, Kirsten stood up, firing around her, and then legged it after them. She would then stop and turn, firing back behind her. There was still gunfire of the unsilenced kind, so at least a few of the Revenge group were still alive. It was a strange

CHAPTER 14

situation. People moving quietly in the dark, or as quietly as they could, and rapid bursts of deadly gunfire.

Where the shots were coming from was difficult to ascertain. Kirsten ran, following in behind Emmett, who was significantly slower than Sabine. She saw Sabine ahead, lift a gun, and fire. She had tagged a man in front of her, but Kirsten saw another one. Running past Emmett, she fired, taking the man off his feet, and then shot the other one.

'Go!' she said to Sabine. 'Go!'

'Where now?'

'Wherever. Do not stop! Do not stop!' Kirsten turned back and grabbed Emmett, hauling him forward. 'Keep going,' she said. She turned around and fired several times, but everyone was now at a distance. They were getting clear.

Gunfire still rang out. It didn't matter, Kirsten kept the others moving. They were at least a half mile away before Kirsten stopped and looked down. She grabbed her phone. 'Signal,' she beamed. She called it in to Macleod.

When she'd finished, from behind her she heard heavy breathing.

'Up,' said Kirsten to Emmett. He looked at her.

'I'm exhausted.'

'Up. If they get done in there, they'll come sweeping for us. We don't want to be here. My car's not that far away. We get in it, we get out of here.'

'What about our car?' asked Sabine. 'It might be closer.'

'You were meant to be here,' said Kirsten. 'I wasn't. My car needs to leave. Let's go.'

Chapter 15

'Good morning, Detective Chief Inspector.'

Macleod looked up as he got out of the car and saw Anna Hunt walking towards him.

'That was quick,' said Macleod. It was six in the morning, and Macleod had not slept. It was still only five hours since the incident at Loch Lee.

'You have to move quick in my business. Detective Inspector,' said Anna, giving a nod to Hope.

'What are you doing here?' Macleod asked. 'I know I informed you, but I expected that—'

'Some of your excellent police force would have been here? No, I kindly stood them down. That's the thing when you're off on special duties,' said Anna. 'You don't get to see what's been relayed through. It was advised to your chief constable that this needed careful handling.'

'Who advised him?'

'I did,' said Anna. 'Kirsten mentioned it to me and—'

'Mentioned it to you? There was an opportunity here to grab some members of both sides. Sometimes that leads back to other places,' said an agitated Macleod.

'Kirsten said it was a trap. Speaking to her and from what I

CHAPTER 15

could gather, I'm in agreement,' said Anna. 'Basically, Clarissa was taken, she was then allowed to escape and to hand over all the information about Bairstow's meeting here. There was a leak that came out of the police force to the Revenge group. I think you need to look at your own house,' said Anna.

'It's not come from my people,' said Macleod. 'Must be higher up.'

'That, of course, is your decision to make,' said Anna. 'But whatever happened, the Revenge group were mobilised to be here. They were allowed to come in, thinking they were going to kill Bairstow. Bairstow sacrificed himself.'

'Really?' said Macleod.

'Do you expect us to just walk away,' said Hope, 'and leave this?'

'No, I don't,' said Anna. 'I will do the forensics here, the photographs. We will make it look as if it's been hushed up.'

'I had Emmett follow two women,' said an angry Macleod, 'who took part in this. He said there were lots of vans that turned up. How do you hush up that many vans?'

'It's a terrible road accident. We're not sure why these people were all together, but they were, and, well, no survivors from the crash. Terrible when you drive down a ravine.'

'You say that too glibly,' said Macleod.

'Just doing my job,' said Anna. 'By hushing this up, we don't let the panic stations go amongst the Forseti group. It worked as they wanted it to. Can you tell me, Seoras, you said you had a farmhouse watched? Anyone come back to it?'

'No one. Perry and Susan have been watching it. When this all happened, I told them to get some people and move in. There's nothing there. Just abandoned. It was just a meeting point. The other cars and that are there.'

'That's okay. That's where they started their trip from, before they ended up in the ravine. That'll work. Would you like to see the scene?'

'I think the word "like" is not appropriate,' said Hope. 'If you'll excuse me a minute.' Anna watched as Hope disappeared off beyond the car and bent down. She could hear her throwing up before she came back.

'Not gone yet,' said Anna.

'Clearly not,' said Hope. 'Look, work to do. Come on.'

Anna Hunt walked Macleod and Hope around Loch Lee and up to the site where the stone circle still was. There were bodies lying here and there, or at least what looked like bodies. Some were being worked on, but most had a camouflage blanket placed over the top of them.

'In case anybody from above sees anything,' noted Anna.

Macleod looked at the ground and saw a gun lying there. 'How do you cover up if that went off?'

'Well, one bright side is that the Forseti group thugs were all using silenced weapons,' replied Anna. 'They'd have got the majority of the shots off. The shots after that? Farmers. Scaring birds in the night.'

'People believe that?' queried Hope.

'If there aren't a lot of bodies to go along with it, people will believe it,' said Anna. ' Easier to believe than a mass gunfight in your scenic beauty spot. Look here!' She walked towards the middle of the stone circle and pulled back a camouflaged cloth. 'Bairstow cut his own throat,' said Anna.

'Emmett said he did it for the king,' said Macleod.

'Yes, Kirsten told me. He brought them all here because he knew that if they saw him, it would be a go. They encircled, saw Bairstow and meant to take him out. The rest of the figures,

CHAPTER 15

however, were mannequins. Then they had a group of thugs behind. I've got two of the thugs. They were paid discreetly. Only contact: Bairstow. They're useless to us.'

Anna picked up her phone and then looked over at Macleod after taking a call. 'I see you invited other people.'

'I didn't know.'

'DI Grump is here. I told them to send him round.'

'He'll have wanted to see it for himself,' said Macleod. 'I told him to get some rest. It was a bit of a horrific night for them.'

'Kirsten said they were holding up pretty well. Grump's got quite a strong disposition on him. They were shot at, out in Spain. I wouldn't underestimate Grump,' said Anna.

Macleod surveyed the scene for another five minutes before Emmett arrived, marching towards the stones.

'Morning,' said Emmett.

'You okay?' asked Macleod.

'Looks very different in the daylight.'

'Come over here a minute,' said Anna. And she pulled back some camouflaged tarpaulin to reveal a body lying there on its back, looking up at the sky. The eyes were still open. Beside it was a gun, but Emmett was staring at the face.

'I recognise him,' said Emmett.

'So you should,' said Anna. 'Ellen McIntosh's eldest son.'

'He would have been at the forefront of the Revenge group,' said Macleod. 'It's his father that was taken out all those years ago. Ellen may have planned stuff, but Ellen would not go out and do this sort of thing. Ellen's too old for that.'

'True,' said Anna Hunt.

'But how did they know?' asked Macleod.

'It's got to be from within the force,' said Anna. 'Clarissa escapes, passes on the details, and this happens.'

'She did indeed pass on the detail,' said Macleod.

'Now you tell me,' said Anna. 'Clarissa Urquhart, hanging up, hands tied on a hook. How do you let her escape? Why do you not watch her? You leave behind information, unguarded, that tells what's going on here. It screams set up. And then the leak comes from the force. They must have known someone on the force is actually working with the Revenge group.'

'But who?' asked Macleod. 'The only people involved in this are my team.'

'Are you sure of them all? How long have you known them? Has any of them got connections to the past?' asked Anna.

'You can stop right there,' said Macleod.

'No, she's right,' said Emmett. 'We have to look.'

'No, we don't,' said Hope. 'We know each other. We know we're good.'

'This is different,' said Emmett. 'We're talking about people that were wronged. We're not just talking about criminals.'

'You're talking about people who almost let some babies get blown up last time,' said Macleod. 'No, we're good.'

'Higher up though, the ACC, the chief constable, they'll know what we were doing,' said Emmett.

'I told Jim,' said Macleod. 'Who knows who he could have told.'

'Food for thought,' said Anna Hunt. 'I'll be clearing all this up very soon. Like I say, clever accident, many bodies down a ravine, we'll put some cover story in, people getting together. If they've all been meeting each other anyway, it will not look that bad. But these random bunch of people are all together.'

'Why are you hushing it up?' asked Macleod.

'I was asked to,' said Anna. 'From up above.'

'And you just do what?' said Macleod. 'Just hush it up?'

CHAPTER 15

'Sometimes I think you don't get the role that I have,' said Anna. 'I don't quite have masters up above me. But the Service operates in this bubble that says you're there to do for the good of the country. Now, when certain people ask, we hush things up, because . . . well look at this. A massacre on a hillside with a stone circle. Screams cult. It screams disaster. It screams everything that there probably actually isn't. We don't want that. So, when they ask me to cover it up, I cover it up, because this being covered up is in the best interest of the country.'

'How do you figure that?' said Macleod. 'We've got people who have basically been set up to be murdered.'

'Indeed,' said Anna. 'Those people have previously murdered other people, and the people who came in to do it have also murdered other people. Can you imagine the press getting hold of this? It's just murder, death everywhere. Macleod's lost control of the whole situation. Murder squads here, there, everywhere. That causes panic. People like to think they're in a safe society.'

'We generally are,' said Hope.

'Indeed,' said Anna. 'But you need the illusion to remain as well. You need the idea in their heads that it is safe, because if it changes in their head, then paranoia breaks out. And things happen, not because of bad people, but because the good people get spooked.'

'And so what? You just do it?' said Macleod.

'Seoras, I just do it, and I cover it up, and I will send all the information from here to you. I will do what you do without the circus. You will have your information to investigate. What I'm saying in the meantime is go back up the road and check your own place. I will also take an interest in all of this, but I will do it on the quiet.

'The position the Service sits in is that the Service can get played. We can get used to cover up things that are not necessarily important for the country. And that's because rich people, important people, do things they shouldn't. Let's not forget the end goal here. The Forseti group.

'Bairstow, as he died, said he was saving the king. Not the monarch, not the one ruling over our country. The king of the Forseti group. That's why he did it. That's why he killed himself. Someone with influence enough to make somebody do that. You look around and you think there's a king. There's a king. This looks like a cult. This isn't a cult. The cult is the Forseti group itself, and the people at the top. And these people need no paraphernalia, need no dress-up. They are a cult. It is a death cult, and it is in our society at the moment,' said Anna. 'And that's where I'm going, for them! And you're going to help me get there,' she said to Macleod.

'I'll have a look, thoroughly search the station, find out what's going on,' said Macleod. 'But this makes the investigation difficult.'

'Because?' said Anna.

'Because of the Revenge group. Look at it. It's been obliterated. You don't come to a party like this. You don't come with the head honcho, McIntosh's eldest son, unless you think you are going for broke.'

'You may be right, but we've still got others to catch. We've still got the Forseti group,' said Anna.

'Previously, they were being hunted,' said Emmett. 'Now they're not. Now they can linger in the shadows again.'

'Doesn't matter,' said Anna. 'If somebody else isn't flushing them out, we might have to. But it doesn't matter. And we keep going because we can't let them rest. They'll be rattled by this. They've lost how many of their group over the last few months? Now's the time.'

Macleod turned away and walked with Emmett and Hope back towards their car. As they got there, Emmett turned to Macleod.

'This could get messy if it's Jim,' said Emmett.

'I don't believe it's Jim,' said Macleod, 'but we'll go through with it. We'll follow through, get everyone together. We'll make a new line of attack.'

'Are you all right?' Hope said to Macleod after Emmett had left for his car.

'We got played,' said Macleod. 'We got played. The Revenge group got played. It's done. The Forseti group is in the place it wanted to be. What bothers me is the way it got rid of the Revenge group. It knows we're still on the case, still coming for it. This is how it will end up for us.'

'Only if we don't get them first,' said Hope.

'We're looking to arrest them. They're not looking to do that with us or anyone else. We're at a clear disadvantage.'

'That's not like you,' said Hope.

'See the bodies out there? It's what I don't want,' said Macleod. 'I trust our people. I also need to make sure I protect them. I'm wondering, is this enough? Maybe we should leave the whole thing to Anna Hunt.'

'Well, not for the moment,' said Hope. 'Let's get back up the road, talk it over. It'll be different when you've got a plan. The rest of them won't want to back out.'

'No,' said Macleod. 'That's why it will be my decision.'

Chapter 16

Macleod stood and looked out his office window. It was getting to be too common an occurrence. Looking out at nothing, struggling to find something to chew over. His coffee cup was in his hand, but the coffee was cold. He couldn't see how to proceed now—how to get around this. And that wasn't like him.

Macleod was used to stepping up, taking charge, moving forward. He did what he had to do and brought the team back together. But he would let Hope drive this. Ask the questions. He knew it had worked well in the past when he stepped to one side and let Hope work with the team. She was good at that. Good at getting close, elucidating information from them. Macleod was aware, at times, some of the team were in awe of him. Some of them were a little intimidated by him, even now. Hope could facilitate better.

He put down the coffee cup with the cold coffee and walked out of his office, telling Tanya he'd be down in Hope's office if needed. He could see the way she looked at him. Not a simple working glance that said 'of course,' but rather with eyes that seemed to almost pity him. He didn't need pitied. He needed to think it out, to get hold of the situation.

CHAPTER 16

Macleod made his way down the stairs, to the floor below and round to Hope's office. The larger office outside was empty. The team had already assembled and, even though he saw them in there, he still knocked the door and waited for a 'come in' from Hope. Rather than walk over beside the screen at the round table, he perched himself on Hope's desk and turned to look at the gathered throng. They were all there, including Kirsten, for this would be the time when they would work out a way forward, and he needed everyone on board for that. He never knew where the inspiration was going to come from.

'We've taken a hit,' said Macleod, standing now, a little shocked. 'The Revenge group has been decimated. Will there be any more of it? We don't know. It all remains to be seen. However, the Forseti group is still at large. We had links into them. We had Bairstow. But Bairstow died a good soldier. We need to know who knew what and when. Need to know where to look next. Hope.'

It was a simple statement. One word asking her to take it forward. And as usual, she stood up, her six feet of height imposing on everyone else, the red ponytail emerging from the back of her head. Yet she looked different, a slight bump around her mid-rift.

'Heads up, everyone,' said Hope. 'We need to know what we really know, not what we think we know. How did the word of Forseti group's meeting get to the Revenge group? They came together, they approached, and walked into a trap. How was the trap set?' Hope stopped abruptly, looking around her, waiting for an answer.

'Given that they used Clarissa to pass out the detail, it must have come from a leak in the force, mustn't it?' said Emmett.

'How else does it get there? I doubt it's anyone in this room. Kirsten will attest. Sabine and I were pinned down. It's only because of Kirsten we walked out.'

'Well, they tried to kill my Frank, as I have since discovered,' said Clarissa, 'so it's not me, and I don't see it being Pats either, or Als for that reason.'

'Well,' said Kirsten, 'it's not come from any of the phones, tablets, computers owned by this group.'

'How do you know that?' asked Hope.

'I went through them, along with Ross.'

Hope glanced over at Ross, and he simply nodded.

'My apologies,' said Kirsten. 'But we had to be sure. I know Seoras vouches for you all. Hope vouches for you all. Clarissa vouches for her team. Everybody vouches for everyone else. But coming from my background, that's not good enough. You check. You check also in case someone's been hacked. Someone is being spied upon. Maybe it's not from this group.'

'It's good to hear,' said Clarissa, 'because they tried to kill my Frank, and I would kill anyone who—'

'Clarissa,' said Macleod, 'I think we all know what you would do. It's not from this room, so let's not get worked up.'

'Not get worked up?' said Clarissa. 'They tried to kill Frank. They would have done, except—'

'Except I put protection on. I asked Anna Hunt to look after people, and she did. Yes, it's not good, but it's done. And it's not anybody in here.'

'I've been thinking about it,' said Perry. 'The napkin. The napkin was a plant. Think about it. They must have sent the hitman in, not believing anyone else was there. And yet, the hitman's found dead with the napkin. The napkin would be dropped deliberately by him. I believe they would have killed

CHAPTER 16

Frank, and had the napkin dropped nearby. And then, we would have investigated. Clarissa, myself, yourself, one of us. Maybe then they would have jumped us. Taken us away. But instead—'

'Instead, Clarissa got into the car boot,' said Macleod. 'Handed herself over on a plate.'

'Exactly,' said Perry, and received a glance like daggers from Clarissa. 'She handed herself over. She gave them what they were intending to do. With Frank dead, Clarissa would have investigated whether or not you wanted her to,' Perry said to Macleod.

'Okay,' said Macleod, 'how does that work then?'

'We were never meant to be following the Revenge group. That was different,' said Kirsten. 'You split the team. You had us going off on different angles. They thought we were after Bairstow, thought Bairstow was the lead. They weren't so sure about the others. There was no way they could know we would get close to the Revenge group. Not the way we did. Not how close we got. Two figures being tailed. Completely different to what they expected.'

'So,' said Hope, 'what should have been the outcome?'

'Well,' said Kirsten, 'we weren't there. We weren't following. Revenge groups arrive. They kill them. Just take them out. Bairstow, a sacrifice in the middle, never intending to walk away. He was told that's what his end would be. To serve his king.'

'So, everything got a bit messed up,' said Macleod. 'If this had have gone to plan, nobody ever would have known about the bodies. They would have disposed of them. The only people who would have known about the plan to get there would have been us. And we would have got to the site. To see what?'

'I think Clarissa got out early,' said Kirsten. 'I think they were hanging her there to wait until it was done, and then she'd get released. They'd make it happen.'

'It's all a bit flimsy,' said Macleod. 'I get the fact we were played, but basing it on Clarissa's ability to free herself. Tell me again what was involved,' Macleod asked Clarissa.

She stood up in her tartan shawl and trousers. 'You've got to imagine me,' said Clarissa, 'in just my underwear.'

Patterson nearly burst out laughing, and Clarissa cut him a look. 'It wasn't nice, Pats. It really wasn't. I had my hands up above my head like this. They're tied, not quite together, but with a band that's now hanging over a hook from the ceiling. To get off, I first tried to get a chair, but I couldn't reach it. I then had to swing. I kept swinging for ages, before I could get enough momentum to lift my hands off and get the bind to clear the hook.'

'Maybe,' said Perry, 'the plan was to drop a hint to where you were later. Then we would have walked in; there would have been the plans, etc. We would have gone.'

'Whoa,' said Macleod. 'That doesn't work. They had to know when the Revenge group was going.'

'So,' said Clarissa, 'they set me up to escape. They knew I would get off that hook. Knew I would find things.'

'They all walked away,' said Kirsten. 'That says that they were planning this. That says they left it open for you to be used to pass the message on.'

'Let's look at the trail,' said Hope, pulling everyone back in together. 'Where did that location go? Clarissa had it first.'

'I told Seoras,' said Clarissa.

'And I told Kirsten. I told Jim,' said Macleod.

'Who did Jim tell?'

CHAPTER 16

'We need to ask,' said Hope. 'Chief Constable, I think. Got to be. Also, Anna Hunt knew the location. We told her.'

'It's not Anna,' said Kirsten. 'Anna doesn't do these things. Anna doesn't work like that. She wouldn't want to roll the Revenge group into a murder like that. Too risky and you can't control it. Not her operating mode. If she'd wanted them dead and she knew who they all were, she'd carry it out herself. It wouldn't have been a killing. She'd have made it look like an accident somewhere. Too many people involved.'

'So this team had it,' said Macleod. 'I don't believe anybody in the team did it. Anna had it. We don't believe Anna did anything with it. Jim had it.'

'And the Chief Constable,' said Perry. 'Can we say that they did nothing with it?'

'No, we can't,' said Hope. 'We clearly can't. We need to talk to Jim and make sure. We also need to talk to Anna Hunt.'

'Told you,' said Kirsten. 'Anna wouldn't do that. Not the way she works.'

'That's you, making a judgement and not knowing for sure,' said Hope.

'I know for sure,' said Kirsten.

'No,' said Macleod. 'Kirsten, if you're going to be involved in this like the rest of us, we make sure. We didn't trust ourselves. At least you didn't. You went and checked.'

'Yes, Kirstie,' said Clarissa. 'We need to check everyone.'

'She killed the guy who was trying to shoot Frank,' said Kirsten.

'Doesn't stop her from taking the opportunity when it comes along,' retorted Patterson.

'That's right, Pats. You can't trust people out there,' said Clarissa. 'Kirstie, we can't just assume—'

'If you don't know your people, you're lost,' said Kirsten.

'Whoa,' said Hope, 'we do this the way we've done it with ourselves. You knew us, yet you still checked. You need to check Anna.'

'Check Anna?' said Kirsten. 'Easier said than done.'

'Well, that's true,' said Macleod, 'and that's why you'll join Hope in going to check Anna.' Kirsten stared at him. 'You know her,' said Macleod. 'I think I know her. You know this team, you know me, you know Hope, you've worked with plenty of us here. Known Ross for how long? That's why you got him to go through the computers with you. And yet you still checked.'

'Checking Anna,' said Kirsten, 'won't be easy.'

'I'm not talking about checking her by breaking into files or anything,' said Macleod. 'You know her well. You can read her. You haven't met her since that night. Talk to her with Hope. You say she's clear after that? I'll go with it. I will also see Jim. Find out where the detail of the location went after that. We go down this line, we find out where it went. And then we act.'

'Hang on a minute,' said Emmett. 'There's another angle. The McIntoshes are clearly involved. We're assuming that this leak came from here. We need to look at the other end. If the McIntoshes got told, if we investigate them, we may find out where it came from. It's the other end of the line.'

Hope stood with her hands on her hips for a moment, looking at Emmett. And then she nodded before looking at Macleod. Macleod looked over at Emmett.

'Take your team to Glasgow. Find out what the McIntoshes are up to. Find out where it came from. They'll be in disarray. Find out if there's still any Revenge group remaining.'

'Yes, sir,' said Emmett. He stood up, looked at Sabine, and

CHAPTER 16

then over at Susan and Perry. The other three stood up as well and followed Emmett out of the room.

'What do I do?' said Clarissa.

'You stay here. You don't go anywhere for a bit. Not until I've spoken to Jim. Then I'll have something for you to do.' Clarissa nodded, stood up with Patterson and Ross, and left the room. It left Macleod, Hope and Kirsten together.

'Anna Hunt. She won't like it,' said Kirsten. 'She won't like you don't trust her.'

'She won't like it, but she will appreciate it,' said Macleod. 'She thinks I'm too trusting to begin with. It's part of the problem. She'll appreciate it because I'm thinking like her. Wondering where it came from, this leak. She'll even put me in the frame, just to check. It's the way you spies work, isn't it?'

'True,' said Kirsten. 'I'll set the meet-up with Anna. I'll call you shortly,' she said to Hope. Kirsten left Hope and Macleod together in the room.

'I don't like this,' said Hope. 'We're questioning ourselves. We're looking inward.'

'Exactly,' said Macleod. 'Keep an open mind. It's too easy to get focused on one issue. Clarissa's under pressure. They tried to kill Frank. She's going to want to have somebody for that. Emmett's doing well, though. Emmett's stepping back.'

'You are too,' said Hope. 'We'll get them. We'll work it out.'

'I hope so,' said Macleod. 'I really hope so.'

Chapter 17

Macleod sat down behind his desk and thought about the call he was about to make. He didn't think it was possible that Jim had sold him out, that he'd passed on information to the Revenge group. And yet when he thought about his character, he would want justice served on the Forseti group. He would want them taken out of the way.

The Forseti group was a stain, much more than the Revenge group. For the Revenge group, they could all understand their motives. Their parents, their uncles, relatives, people had been killed. And although they were criminals, you could understand the hatred and the desire to get back at what they would have seen as authorities. Jim wanted the Forseti group out of the way, and so had the Chief Constable.

He didn't think the Chief Constable was a political person. The man always seemed to be non-partisan when it came to politics, which was not always the case with previous incumbents.

Macleod also thought about where he should meet Jim. If he was going to put him under a little pressure, better to do it in this office than any other. He pressed his button for Tanya

CHAPTER 17

to come and see him.

There was a knock at the door ten seconds later. Macleod said to come in and Tanya entered.

'Can you get Jim on the line to me? No, rather, ask him to come down,' said Macleod. 'Invite him in here. I'll need coffee and that. The usual. Once he's in, I don't want to be disturbed. I don't want anybody near that door. Do you understand?'

'Absolutely,' said Tanya. 'I'll make sure it's clear on the floor. No one gets beyond my desk.'

'Good,' said Macleod. 'Thank you.'

Macleod picked up a pen and started tapping it. He wasn't a man prone to nerves, but this was going to be an awkward conversation. It was one he wasn't looking forward to.

Ten minutes later, there was a knock at the door. Macleod said to come in, and Tanya opened it and presented the Assistant Chief Constable. She said she'd be back with the coffee in a minute.

Jim stepped forward, sitting down in a seat in front of Macleod. Macleod thought about going to the sofa in the far corner but he wanted the conversation to sound formal. He wanted to make it seem that he was almost making an accusation. He wanted Jim under pressure.

He could tell a lot about people when they were under pressure. He could tell a lot by the way they reacted. Macleod was good at that. He'd seen people over the years; he knew how people hid away; could see the true reactions and feelings go somewhere else.

Tanya brought the coffee in, and when normally Macleod would have said he would have poured, he let Tanya stay pouring the coffee in silence until she was ready to leave the room. Once she'd shut the door behind her, Macleod leaned forward on his desk.

'We've got a problem, Jim.'

'What sort of a problem?' Jim asked, taking his coffee.

'We've got a leak.'

'What do you mean?'

'Clarissa got held. Clarissa was in a situation where she found information. It was fed back into the force. Came to my team. It came to me. It went to you. Where did it go after you?'

'You think that I leaked it?' spat Jim.

'I didn't say that. I asked where it went after you.'

'The chief constable,' said Jim.

'Why?' asked Macleod.

'He wanted to stay in the loop. He's the chief constable. I can tell him things.'

'Who else knows what I'm doing at the moment?' asked Macleod.

'You know who knows,' said Jim. 'Me, chief constable, you, and any of your team that you choose to advise.'

'So, a leak can only come from either my team, me, yourself, or the chief constable. Has he passed it on anywhere else, the chief constable?'

'He's solid; you know that. He's not one of them.'

'But this killing, it didn't start off as a killing of the Revenge group. It started off with the Revenge group thinking they were going to kill one of the principal men in the Forseti group. It was a ruse to bring them in. That suggests somebody knew there was a spy. And I missed somebody passing information.'

'And you think it was me?' said Jim.

'No,' said Macleod, 'I don't think.'

'What about your people? Guys don't earn much . . . maybe

CHAPTER 17

something in their pocket.'

'No, and besides, we checked. We've gone through everybody's records. We've gone through all their phone calls, their laptops.'

'Well, people could always turn around and get another laptop, use something else,' said Jim.

'It's true,' said Macleod. 'But the time involved, the speed, the way in which it arrived. Suddenly everyone's on the move. They've got a gathering and they're going to attack Bairstow with everything they've got. The big moment, chance for someone important, really important.'

'There is that,' said Jim. 'I'll hand that to you. But it's not me.'

'You happy for us to take your computer, your phone?'

'It's got stuff on it you're not meant to be privy to. Now you say you looked into your own team,' said Jim. 'Have you gone beyond their computers and laptops? Have you gone to look at where they were and what they were doing?'

'I've got a team of four and a team of three. They're intermixed. They're all over the place at the moment. This would not be a team you could run a leak from.'

'I think you underestimate people,' said Jim. 'I think there's plenty of people who could run it like that.'

'It's not my team,' said Macleod, 'which doesn't leave a lot of options.'

'Am I being accused here?' said Jim. 'Do I need to get a lawyer in?'

'Chief Constable. We need to know.'

'Well, bring him down then,' said Jim. 'I organised this task force. I pushed for it from the Chief Constable.'

'All the more reason then, pushing to help the Revenge group bring out the Forseti group.'

'I am no leak. I would not do that. And I certainly would not approve of the Revenge group going in and just killing them. It needs justice, it needs jail terms.'

'Maybe so,' said Macleod.

'Just maybe so.' Jim stood up. 'You'd better get to the bottom of this. And you're going to find who's really done it. I thought there was a bit of trust going on here, Seoras. I thought we were actually working together. And now you're not even sure I'm on the same team. You can keep your damn coffee.'

Jim stood up, spun on his heel, left the room, slamming the door behind him. There was a rap about ten seconds later. 'Come in,' said Macleod. Tanya entered, looking at him cautiously.

'Are you sure you're doing the right thing here?' asked Tanya.

'Get me Clarissa!'

'Of course,' said Tanya, and left. She came back in with Clarissa and left her with Macleod.

'Are you ready?' asked Macleod. 'I need you to make a real difference and do something very tough.'

'What?' asked Clarissa.

'The trail says that Jim had the information, and then he passed it to the chief constable. So, either of them could have passed on the information about the location of the Forseti group's ritual. We need to find out who, Clarissa.'

'You want me to tail the chief constable? I don't know if you noticed, Seoras, I'm actually one of the more obvious people.'

'You're also somebody who can operate around the bigwigs. Chief constable has meetings with very senior people. You could charm your way into anything, and if not, you can fight and kick hard. You also won't be behind the door in actually bringing justice if needs be.'

CHAPTER 17

'Tell me, you really think he's guilty?'

'We don't have any evidence. We don't know who passed it on. At the moment, I'm actually second-guessing ourselves. Did we drop it somehow? Are we being tapped? Are we being looked into? I've got nothing. Understand that, Clarissa. We've got nothing. I said we were going to launch a task group, and now I'm sitting with a lot of dead bodies. The only saving grace is that Anna cleaned it up. And even that, I don't know if it's a saving grace or just Anna covering her tracks.'

'What's your gut say?' asked Clarissa.

'What?'

'Your gut. Your old Macleod gut's never a bad thing to go by.'

'My gut says there's something fishy going on, something not right. I just don't like the way everything's come together, it's too, well, it just doesn't sit.'

'You want me to cover them both?' asked Clarissa.

'Chief constable especially. Jim, I don't think it's him, but sometimes you don't know people.'

Clarissa looked at the table in front of her. There was a cup of coffee. 'Oh, that's kind of you,' she said.

'Jim's, he walked out and left it behind.'

'What, I thought you two were getting on all right?'

'I had to play hardball, to see the reaction.'

'I'll stick Ross on Jim. Ross is thorough, incredibly polite. He'll look good being close and around. He'll always have an excuse. And besides, Jim doesn't handle the fact that Ross has got a male partner. It's good for the press, but he's never really liked it, has he?'

'No,' said Macleod.

'Well, I'll use that prejudice against him. He's less likely to question Ross, whereas, he'll question me all day long. He doesn't like me either, but that's his problem if he doesn't like Tartan.' She gave a smile and stood up to leave. But then stopped. 'I don't think this gets you off the hook.'

'Off the hook?' said Macleod.

'You brought Jim in, gave him coffee, and all you were doing was shaking him down. You're actually asking me for to go above and beyond, and there's no coffee. Slack, Seoras. Slack.'

'Before you go,' said Macleod. 'Are you all right?'

'What do you mean, all right?' asked Clarissa.

'They held you. You must have thought you might have been dead. You must have—'

Clarissa walked to the door, checked to see if anybody was behind it, and then came back to the table where Macleod pressed the button on his intercom. 'Tanya! Make sure nobody comes into this office until I say.'

Tanya answered in the affirmative. Clarissa gave a nod. 'They hung me up, Seoras. I was in my underwear. They might have found that funny downstairs, but I didn't. One of them, he threatened to, well, he threatened to remove it. You remove those and what's next? I didn't want to know what was next. I'm not in any sort of shape to kick back, to fight. Not like I used to.'

'He actually threatened to do that?' said Macleod.

'I haven't told Frank,' said Clarissa.

'Does Frank know about the gunman?'

'No,' said Clarissa.

'These are serious dangers,' said Macleod. 'He should know what you're getting into. Not the detail, just the likelihood of something.'

'Likelihood, is it? You think it likely?'

CHAPTER 17

'You know as well as I do, the potential, what can go wrong.' Macleod stood up, walked round the table, and came over to Clarissa.

'What?' she said.

'I'm sorry. I'm sorry you get called in like that. I'm sorry I got you back on this. You walked away from the murder team. You walked away from—'

'Enough,' she said. 'I got myself involved. I went through to Helgoland for you. And these bastards tried to kill babies. And the other side just wants to kill anyone. Random execution. I am in, and I know there's cost and there are consequences. But I'm in. I'm one of your DIs. I'm not the little DC running around, getting told what to do. But nobody deserves what those little ones nearly got. Even to think what might have happened to them.'

He reached forward and Clarissa let him hug her. 'I'm glad you're safe,' he whispered in her ear. When the hug broke, Clarissa turned and walked to the door. She looked back at him. 'You're going soft.'

'I thought it would actually be easier,' he said. 'I am now the DCI. But I've got the three of you. I've got the teams under you. You're my people. Anything that happens to any of you, I feel it, Clarissa. You don't believe it, but I do.'

'I'll go see the chief constable. I'll let you know if I think there's something wrong.'

'Thank you,' said Macleod. 'Be thorough, but no risks. It's the chief constable. Your career could be on the line.'

'Screw the career. I've got Frank at home. We've got pensions. We'll get by.'

Macleod smiled at her.

'Still, take care. And watch out for Ross too. If it is an inside leak, you may get an enemy coming to you looking like a friend.'

'I've been with Kirsten,' said Clarissa. 'Kirsten taught me a few things, and I was a hard nut job before that.'

She closed the door, and Macleod simply stared at it and laughed. Of all the police officers he'd worked with, Clarissa was unique. Something else in the extreme. But he wasn't sure what.

Chapter 18

'Just pull up there,' said Kirsten. Hope turned the car in, applied the handbrake, and then looked at Kirsten.

'I am aware. You realise I've met her before?'

'I've not just met her. I've worked with her,' said Kirsten. 'Let me make the call. Let me decide if she's holding anything back.'

'You know Macleod didn't put me in here as a chauffeur? He didn't say you're my number two to you. You look after the team and run it. He didn't say to me, go home and have your family. What are you doing out here? I don't need you.'

'So why am I here then, if you're that wonderful?' said Kirsten.

Hope stopped for a minute, turned and looked at Kirsten. She wondered for a moment, but as the woman got out of the car, it clicked with her. All those years ago, Kirsten had been that special one, with Macleod. He had seen that she thought like him. She was a protégé.

Hope never was the protégé. Hope was the one he enjoyed working with. Kirsten had then moved on, come back, and the old boss had needed her out in Italy. Honestly, he needed her now, and yet Hope was still his go-to. Hope was still the one he would rely on to look after everyone else.

Hope wondered if Kirsten wasn't a little jealous. She could understand. The woman had lost her love as Hope understood it; therefore, she was looking for the next love of her life. Macleod wasn't quite that, but he was her mentor. He was more than what Anna Hunt was to her, despite all the spy craft they shared. Anna had been her mentor out in the Service and now they were going to question that mentor. Macleod had insisted on it. More than that, he hadn't trusted Kirsten to simply go out there. He wanted Hope to do it because he was feeling uneasy.

Hope stepped out of the car and followed Kirsten. The small wooden table beside Loch Ness was the venue once again, and today the sun was shining. There were indeed some tourists nearby, but Anna stood up, smiling, as the pair of women approached her.

'Meeting again so soon? I'd have thought you wouldn't have had time to be busy. I thought there was plenty to do in hunting down this leak.'

'We're back to work,' said Hope. 'I'd like to know what you knew—'

'Excuse me?' said Anna.

'I'd like to know what you knew about that location, prior to when Macleod passed it to you.'

'I told them,' said Kirsten. 'I told them that—'

Anna put her hand up. 'I'm beginning to like you,' she said to Hope. 'Few people would have had the balls to come and say that straight out. Macleod teach you that one?'

'What's the answer?' asked Hope.

'I didn't have any location information. Not until Macleod passed it. He said to me, Kirsten was going. It all sounded

CHAPTER 18

good. I held back until assistance was required. Once I heard it had all gone to, well, rats, that's when I moved. If we knew there was a dispatching of the Revenge group, and the Forseti group were still there, I'd have let you sort it. But I got a call afterwards from higher-up people, decent people, who said that things couldn't be said. Things couldn't be let out. I needed to do a clean-up operation. So that's what I did. I cleaned it up. Then I got more involved.'

'I'm trying to see the angle where you benefit from this,' said Hope. 'Other than the Revenge group is gone. You still have the top people unknown; you still have the Forseti group active. I don't see you as being someone comfortable with them being out there. You'd want them sorted; you'd want them taken down.'

'Unstable, that's what you're trying to say,' said Anna. 'You're right; they're an unstable group and we need them gone. I don't need pressure from people with their own agendas. Government pressure? Pressure from people who think they know the best for the nation, even if they don't, fine. We can handle people who are making the best of calls, even though their judgement sometimes is askew, either because they don't know all the facts or because they just don't make very good judgements. We can handle that. People with their own agendas calling shots higher up, I'm not comfortable with.'

'Speaking of which,' asked Hope, 'do you know of any leaks from the force?'

'Sit down,' said Anna. 'I have coffee.'

Hope sat down, but Kirsten didn't.

'You can sit,' said Hope.

'She's not happy,' said Anna. 'Hope, you're an excellent operator, but sometimes you miss the nuances higher up.

Kirsten's annoyed because Macleod sent you and her. That's what's bugging you, Kirsten?' asked Anna.

Kirsten gave a grunt and then sat down beside Hope as Anna poured coffee.

'There's no room for that,' Anna said. 'When you get to the top, Kirsten, when you have to make the compromises, when you have to understand that you don't know everything and you're not the best, then sometimes you have to use other people, sometimes people you're jealous of.'

Kirsten grunted again and looked away.

'Don't be like that,' said Anna. 'It's Macleod's fault.'

'What do you mean?' asked Hope.

'He's incredibly endearing, isn't he? You want to help him. You want to get there because he's such a thoroughly decent man. Even with all this going on, he wants to arrest this group. Kirsten's struggling with that now. Best thing to do would be identify them and take them down. Take them to court with their clout? Right. Are you ever going to get a conviction?'

'That's who he is.'

'Yes, it is. And it draws you to him. The decency. Let's be honest; we've all felt it—all three of us. That's why we still work around him.'

Hope could feel herself becoming a little flushed, and Anna watched her face. 'Bit of a glow from the pregnancy,' said Anna.

'That's very kind,' said Hope. 'But I'm taking your point. Do you know of anyone within the force, though? Anything that's been going on? Any potential leaks?'

'I haven't got anything,' said Anna. 'One of my list of problems. It's why I'm hoping Macleod will come up with things. I've told him before. The Service isn't in great shape at the moment. I'm having to re-recruit; I'm having to sort things

CHAPTER 18

out. Could do with that woman there being back alongside me, but he taught her too damn well.'

'The Service manipulates you. The Service requires compromise to a point where I won't go,' said Kirsten.

'Nonsense. You left because you got hurt and you got hurt bad. And I get that,' said Anna, 'but don't throw this nonsense back at me. You wanted out; you stayed out. You're coming in and doing the right thing and helping out, great, but every day you stay away from us, it's a day we lose someone of your calibre and somebody else goes free.'

Kirsten glared for a moment and Hope felt the need to interject. 'No need for tension at the moment,' said Hope. 'We're all on the same side.'

'Are you sure?' said Anna. 'That's why you came here. You came to find that out.'

'And we are,' said Hope. 'I can read it from you.'

'I'm a spy. I can pull the wool over people's eyes.'

'No,' said Hope. 'You want this done and you need it done right. If you weren't that decent person, if there wasn't that bit of Macleod inside you, you wouldn't be here talking to us. You wouldn't have been talking to him. You haven't brought him in because of some sort of fondness; you've brought him in because you know he can get to the bottom of this, and at the moment you're struggling. But he'll also follow a rightness, one that you have.'

'You're saying Macleod and I are the same?' asked Anna.

'Oh no,' said Hope. 'You'll go to more extremes. You see a fairness in people being removed because you can't get them in front of a judge. He'll never see that. You probably see it as one of his weaknesses.'

'And you probably see it as one of his strengths,' said Anna.

'No,' said Hope. 'I don't. I will follow the law. I will go by the book. But when the book doesn't work, I'm perfectly open to the idea somebody else is going to have to deal with it.'

Anna grinned at her. 'It's a shame about your baby.'

'What do you mean?' asked Hope.

'You could be good for the Service, but your baby will compromise you. I heard they do that.'

'Shame,' said Hope, smiling. But it really wasn't to her.

'The Chief Constable. What do you know about him?' asked Hope.

'What's going on with him? The chief constable is remarkably detached from political figures,' said Anna. 'Remarkably so. It's refreshing. It's great. But you have to understand that this has been a major win for the Forseti group. They may have been trying to bring the Revenge group more into the open. This may be a drive to scupper any links they have with the force, for there may be someone there. In fact, I believe there is someone there. And the Forseti group has simply used Clarissa to highlight that and bring it out.'

'There is the "king" comment, isn't there?' said Kirsten.

'It's always been my idea that there's a central figure trying to run an operation of this size. The secrecy with a council just doesn't work. It sounds great in practice, but it leaves you very exposed. Someone at the top, someone of quality at the top can run these and keep everything intact and when part of the organisation gets discovered they can cut it off quickly.

'Bairstow was in that line and was becoming a problem. Bairstow realised it himself and he cut himself off and took down most of their enemies with it. He was a very high-up figure, I tell that when you spoke to him. Bairstow must have been close. Somebody further up wouldn't have operated like this, wouldn't have looked to go out in a blaze of glory. It'll run the further you get into an organization, the more belief you have in it.

'But he killed himself,' said Hope. 'Obedience to the point where he killed himself to protect—'

'To protect what?' asked Anna. 'To protect somebody else? No, this is a cult. It may look like an organisation but it's a cult. And that's why someone like Bairstow operates in this fashion.'

'But he took an order.'

'I'm not even sure he did,' said Anna. 'Bairstow will probably have set this all up. That's the way they'll do it. Bairstow will have come. He'll have said, "I'll set this up." And he'll have said goodbye. And then, when he dies with it, the only links come out of Bairstow. Nothing above. There's nowhere to go. There's nothing to find.'

'Except this leak,' said Kirsten.

'Indeed, except this leak.'

'That bothers me,' said Hope. 'From what you're saying about them, the idea that there was a leak left behind bothers me.'

'Well, it's there,' said Anna. 'It's there, in black and white. Somebody leaked. Somebody told them. And the Revenge group found the location and walked into the trap. Bairstow or someone within the Forseti group knew that someone up there was passing on information. It makes sense to how the Revenge group was operating before, how it was able to do things.'

'It understood what we were at,' said Hope.

'Well, it was feeding in, wasn't it?' said Anna. 'The Revenge group was the one who was trying to direct you and move you along. How do you do that if you don't understand the inner workings? Somebody up there must have been doing it.'

'I think you're right,' said Kirsten.

Hope drank her coffee. Decaf. She wished it was caffeine at the moment. In fact, she wished it was a beer or something else. If he wasn't buying this, it sounded good. It sounded like something you could believe if you stumbled upon it. But why would you leave that link? Bairstow was better than that, surely. Wasn't he?

Chapter 19

Ellen McIntosh sat in the back of the black funeral car, her face covered by a veil. Alongside her sat the second of her sons. The first was a few cars behind, inside a wooden box. As Emmett and Sabine watched the funeral from a distance, they noted the enormity of it.

The McIntoshes had been a criminal enterprise in Glasgow before the Forseti group had taken them down. Whether everybody here was an actual criminal, they had certainly turned out to show respect to what was now a depleted crime family. Emmett had called his colleagues in Glasgow to ask about their interview with Ellen McIntosh on hearing of her son's death—a tragic coach accident, several minibuses having fallen down a ravine.

Emmett, of course, knew the actual truth, and he suspected that Ellen McIntosh did as well. She had, however, given no such indications during the police interview with her, simply telling them she now had only the one son. The officer who had conducted the interview had said she was distraught.

And as Emmett looked now at the broken figure inside the black funeral car, he could see that she was struggling to keep her bearing in public. Emmett moved a little closer to see if he could get a better look at the woman, as she entered the church. He stopped in a crowd two deep, close to the steps up to the church, and watched as she was escorted out of the funeral car. Her younger son held her arm, and as she walked, Emmett wondered if she would collapse. She looked up, scanning the crowd, and then to Emmett's horror, made a beeline towards him. The crowd parted, and she stopped, staring straight at Emmett. For a moment she leaned in towards Emmett, whispered something, and then resumed her progress to the church doors.

'What did she say?' asked Sabine.

'She told me she'd find out whoever betrayed him. Told me to tell Macleod she'd kill whoever it was.'

'Well, that's understandable,' said Sabine.

'Yes, but she's also marked my card, hasn't she? How many people just saw my face there? Police officer.'

'You're safe enough here. They must be thinking the police are watching this, left, right, and centre.'

'You mean there's more than us here?' said Emmett, and gave a smile.

'You know there is.'

Sabine looked around and on the far side of the car park stood a rather dishevelled man. He wore a suit jacket that was black, half undone, and partly covered a crooked black tie. You might have thought he'd just appeared from the pub, realising it was late for the funeral, but Perry was intently studying the crowd. The funeral was too big for everyone to be inside the church, and Perry had taken up a position away from Emmett and Sabine. Susan Cunningham was standing a short distance away from Perry, looking much neater, but also taking in what was happening.

CHAPTER 19

The funeral service was relayed from inside and was conducted in an atmosphere of respect. When the coffin came out, heads were bowed, and it was loaded into another funeral car before being driven off for a private burial. The mourners dissipated and Emmett received some hard stares as people walked past him. But he also noticed that Perry was approaching.

This wasn't part of their protocol. Perry would remain aloof, then rendezvous with Susan at their car and meet up with Emmett afterwards. But Perry was coming close to him, staring in a similar fashion to the rest of the mourners. As he walked past Emmett, he said faintly, 'Seen someone. Going to make contact. Catch you later.'

Emmett gave a gentle nod and Perry walked on past. The crowd had moved away, and Emmett looked over at Susan. She was turning to walk to the car, but she gave a quick thumbs up to him. Attending funerals was funny, thought Emmett. He always wanted something shocking to happen, especially as an investigator. You were always looking for that bit of anger to flare up. What had he got?

Well, he'd been identified to most of Ellen McIntosh's crowd, which was clever. Other than that, he'd been told exactly what he knew. Ellen wasn't done with this. She'd be coming for whoever had laid the plans to kill her eldest son.

Emmett turned with Sabine and walked back to the car. They'd had a rather fruitless funeral in terms of the investigation.

* * *

Perry was shambling along, having to step it up to keep contact with the man he wanted to see. He wouldn't grab him in the middle of the crowd. He'd tail him for a bit, wait until he was on his own, and then speak to him. That was because he was a police officer Perry recognised from Glasgow, and he must be on the team that was watching the McIntoshes. It was a crime family. There would always be eyes on them, especially with what happened recently. While Glasgow wasn't on great terms with the Inverness team, Perry knew this man personally. He was decent. He'd talk to him on the quiet.

He watched as the man jumped on a bus and made his way up to the top deck and then to the front. Perry raced and jumped on the bus just in time, paid his fare, and then followed the man up the stairs to spot him sitting at the front of the bus. Perry shuffled along, spied the empty seat behind him, and slid in.

'Don't look round,' said Perry casually. 'How are you doing, Keir? You keeping okay?'

'Warren bloody Perry,' said the man quietly. 'You're causing some ruckus.'

'You know me, Keir. I don't cause a ruckus. I just find it.'

'Saw you at the funeral. Was that blonde with you? The one I saw you arrive with?'

'That's my new partner,' said Perry.

'Wow. You did well there.'

'I'm not here to discuss Susan,' said Perry, mainly because he would have to agree with Keir's assessment. And knowing himself, Perry would bring up all the fact that Tanya was after him, too.

'Tanya went north. She's up working with your guy, isn't she? PA for him. Stepped out of HR.'

'That's right,' said Perry. 'Does everybody know about us

CHAPTER 19

down there?'

'You guys kicked up a heck of a stink.'

'There was a stink to be kicked up,' said Perry.

'Oh, don't,' said Keir. 'Rattled a few faces. Rattled a few people. I wouldn't say you're unpopular, but I wouldn't say you should come to the Christmas do either.'

'I've been down,' said Perry, 'several times. I know where I'm standing at the moment. Can you tell me something?' asked Perry.

'I don't know. Depends what you're asking?'

Perry breathed in deeply. Keir was one of those people who disappeared into a crowd. He was of average height, had an average haircut. His hair was brown, and it was trimmed neatly. But there was nothing shocking about it. His nose was a touch flat. His lips slightly pursed. And his cheeks were heading towards being full and rounded. But his face was forgettable. Perry felt bad thinking about someone in that way, but the man was perfect for undercover work. He was hard to recall. Even for a police officer, in terms of undercover work, he was perfect.

'I take it you've got eyes on the McIntoshes. You know that, well, it wasn't the ravine crash, was it?'

'They reckon there's a group that took them out. Some of it was shut down from above. Rumour says you guys from up north are involved, but they shut down all serious investigations into it round the stations. Possibly bigger than that, though, as far as I understand. This recent death of the eldest McIntosh, it's shrouded in mystery. We think the Service was involved and that's never good. We can't get much information out of the McIntoshes. Some poor sod had to go in and talk to Ellen McIntosh about how her son died in a ravine. I think she told him flat out what she thought of it. Not that it made it into the official report.'

'The older McIntosh. What was he like?'

'Stu McIntosh died, and the business got taken over by those who remained. Now Ellen ran it for a long time but Ellen's not someone who goes out to people. Ellen was very much a figurehead. Clever woman. Very clever. She could work people out. But to enforce it, she would use her boys.

'Now she always looked to pass things down. And the elder one, he was the one she was passing most of it to. The younger son was a lackey to the first one. The elder boy backed her up on everything. He was the one who took Ellen's plans and enforced them. She groomed him into the role for the family. She did incredibly well because they were cut down. You remember it, Perry. All of them. That used to be a heck of a crime family. It's not what it was today. It's not up to those heights. But they've got up and working again.'

They've got up and working a lot more than you realise, Keir, Perry thought. But he would not give that away.

'Have there been any weapon shipments around the family?' asked Perry.

'Rumours. Rumours of weapons dealers, rumours of drugs, rumours of a lot of things. Haven't really been able to get hard evidence, especially with Ellen. Ellen doesn't get her feet wet. Ellen sat back and let the young lad do it.'

'So, what happens now?' asked Perry. 'With the eldest one gone, does she lean on the younger one?'

'I wouldn't think so, or at least I doubt it. You see, they never got on. They never saw eye to eye, the younger one and Ellen. There are rumours she would cut his money when he was younger. She wasn't giving him part of the business. Gave it to a lieutenant, rather than her sons. Stu wouldn't have done that. But then again, Stu McIntosh was a right bastard. If his son wasn't up to it, he'd have cut him loose. And not in the sense of kick him out, he'd have cut him. Disposed of him.'

'His own son?'

'Yes,' said Keir. 'Take care. I knew him fairly well. I wasn't sad to see him go down or any of the rest of them.'

'Has there been anybody else around them? Anybody else of note seen around the family?'

'Not really. You know they have a strip club. At least the older son did.'

'Yes,' said Perry. 'I've been there.'

'Any good?' asked Keir.

'Wasn't really my cup of tea.'

'No, you're classier than that, Perry, aren't you? You always tried to fit in with the lads, but you were a cut above us. That brain of yours.'

'I've quit the cigs, though.'

'You've quit the cigs? I thought I couldn't smell you,' said Keir. And there was silence for a moment. 'Is that for a woman?'

Perry couldn't answer, but he could almost feel Keir grinning. 'That was your trouble Perry, women. You didn't treat them properly; you let them influence the way you were all the time. You should have been more like me. A woman needs to know her place, needs to understand her part of the relationship. She's not there to change the man; she's there to assist him; she's there to give to the relationship.'

'You still divorced, Keir?'

'Twice divorced,' said Keir.

'Well, I'll look for some advice on women elsewhere.'

Keir laughed. 'You might be wise. I've never understood

them. They've never understood me.'

'I'll see you around,' said Perry, and pressed the red button, indicating the bus should stop at the next bus stop.

'Take care of yourself up there,' said Keir. 'And Perry, it will cool down in Glasgow. It'll take them time, but they'll come round to you. Most people liked you.'

'And I like most people,' said Perry. 'Take care of yourself.'

Perry turned and walked down the aisle of the bus before descending the stairs. He had to hold on tight as the bus swung going round a corner and then came to a stop. Perry got out, looked around, and saw a coffee shop. He walked over, purchased a coffee, and sat down. He would need to call Susan to come pick him up, and he wondered exactly where he was. Perry knew Glasgow pretty well, but he hadn't been watching.

Still, he wouldn't call right away. Perry sipped his coffee and then he began to work out where this would go. Ellen McIntosh had lost her son. She was raging. Somebody had betrayed them. Someone had passed on the message. Ellen thought they'd been betrayed. How did she know there was the leak? Did she know her son had somebody on his books? Were the police talking to him? Or maybe they were talking directly to Ellen herself. How did the Forseti group know that, though? How had they engineered this whole situation?

Perry sat back, sipping his coffee. He couldn't see it at the moment, but he would. He always did.

Chapter 20

DS Alan Ross was not happy. He'd been sent on his own to tail his Assistant Chief Constable, a task he wasn't comfortable with. It was one thing to tail other suspects, but to tail one of your bosses seemed wrong. But things were wrong.

Macleod had questioned Jim's integrity, a giant step back after saying previously that he trusted him, and was now saying the team should trust no one. Alan didn't like this. The team was built on trust. They relied on each other. It was all about each other. And then Kirsten had asked him to delve into other people's computers and files.

He'd known they were all okay. It was the only reason he'd done it, because he knew. But Kirsten had changed from that young girl who had started with them. She was now a mature woman, suspicious, thoroughly professional, incredibly strong, and strong-willed with it.

Alan wondered where he had gone in that time. He'd started off as the detective constable, along with Macleod and Hope. Now he was a sergeant. He didn't feel he'd progressed wonderfully. He was getting called to do more and more stuff like this, pulled away from what he enjoyed with the computers.

Alan loved digging for evidence. He didn't enjoy being out and interviewing people. It wasn't him.

He liked running the team from the background, organising them, but Hope was far more organised than Macleod ever was. Even now, despite being pregnant. And then he'd been moved over to work, in this case, with Clarissa. He'd worked with her for a short time on the murder team. She was hard to manage.

She called him 'Als.' He was Ross. Good, solid, dependable Ross. Macleod knew that. Hope called him Alan, and he tolerated that because she was of a more friendly disposition. It helped her, and she didn't call him it in front of other people, generally just when they were on their own. There was a formality needed in the police, one that was getting eroded, and he felt that following his own ACC was a further step on that downward path.

That being said, Ross was bothered because he was sitting in a car watching the Assistant Chief Constable getting out of his own car and approaching a warehouse on an industrial estate. The warehouse used to house a packaging company, but they were ten years gone and the building was in disrepair. This particular estate needed a revamp because most of the warehouses were empty. But it bugged Ross—why would Jim be here?

He watched Jim get to the gates and open them easily, for they were unlocked. As he approached the building, Ross got out of the car and raced over to the gates as Jim went inside. Ross went through and got to the main door that Jim had gone through. It was then he heard somebody walking along the street.

The woman was attractive, Ross would say. He wasn't

CHAPTER 20

someone who could comment on how women stimulated men. But she was attractive in all the classical senses. She had blonde hair flowing down her back. She had red lipstick on, coupled with a long overcoat that wrapped up around what must have been a reasonably sympathetic figure.

Her high heels clicked along, and that's what alerted Ross, forcing him around the corner of the building. He watched her carefully from his obscured vantage point as she approached the main door, a door he had been standing in front of moments ago. She went inside, and Ross wondered if he should follow.

His problem was the door could lead to anywhere. It could be a room that Jim and this woman were now standing in. It could lead to other corridors. He didn't know, and he thought it was not worth the risk. It was suspicious enough, what was going on.

Ross was disappointed he hadn't got a photograph of her on the way in, but the camera was back in the car. He could use his phone, but it was awkward. From such a hidden position, the phone's camera would be at a disadvantage compared to a real camera. He could give a description, but she wasn't someone he recognised from the case.

Ross tucked himself behind the corner as he heard the door open. Carefully, he watched the back of the woman disappearing out of the gates. She didn't look back once, and calmly walked off in the direction she'd come from. Ross held his ground. He watched as Jim then emerged two minutes later. He was holding an envelope and quickly tucked it away inside his coat as he left the building.

Ross began to panic. Jim's car wasn't that far away. He could get in and just drive off. And so, Ross turned, looked around the compound of the building and saw part of the fence out of Jim's view. He ran over, climbed it, dropped onto the other side and ran back towards his car. Ross had just about got into it when Jim drove away.

The Assistant Chief Constable made his way back to the Inverness station and Ross parked up his car as well. Ross went to his own office, but then popped down to the canteen. It was easier to watch someone leave from the canteen, and he couldn't very well go up and ask if Jim was doing anything, or what were his plans for the day. He had, however, alerted Tanya, because Jim's office was on the same floor as Macleod's, and Jim had to walk past Tanya every time he left it to go somewhere.

As he sat down with a coffee in the canteen, he saw a text message from Tanya saying that Jim was in his office. That was something. At least Ross could relax for a bit. But he was agitated. Jim had taken an envelope from a blonde woman. Who was she? Ross had no idea.

Ross was chewing this over as Hope entered the canteen. She gave him a smile, picked up an orange juice, and came and sat beside him.

'Are you okay, Alan?' she asked.

'The Assistant Chief Constable's upstairs in his office. I'm just biding my time. Clarissa and Patterson are down in Glasgow to see the chief constable.'

'You look agitated,' said Hope.

'Just been out on an industrial estate, and the ACC was delivered an envelope by a blonde-haired woman at an abandoned warehouse. He's come back to the station now.'

'Well, that doesn't sound good,' said Hope.

'No, seems very suspicious. Very suspicious,' said Ross. 'If it's

CHAPTER 20

him that has been leaking, well, I don't know what to believe. I don't know what to say. It's like, it's nearly like the DCI doing it,' said Ross.

'Sometimes you get bad eggs,' said Hope.

'The boss didn't think he was a bad egg.'

'The boss is doing what the boss needs to do,' said Hope. 'You did what you had to do when you looked up all about us with Kirsten. We have to be in a different mindset here. A completely different mindset.'

'How are you feeling at the moment?' asked Ross suddenly.

'Still got the nausea,' said Hope.

'No, not like that. I mean about John. The boss said that we would have protection and Anna Hunt was providing it from the Service. But they got so close to Frank. Clarissa was really shaken up by that.'

'As I think any of us would be,' said Hope. 'I don't like it at the moment. I don't like the thought of John being there without me.'

'Me neither,' said Ross. 'Angus and Daniel. They don't deserve any of this coming at them. I mean, a hitman? A hitman to take out Clarissa's partner?'

'It's strange,' said Hope. 'Sometimes you feel like there are rules. It's us and the bad guys. But then, there aren't rules, are there? And these guys at the top, this Forseti group, are almost worse than the criminals we deal with.'

'I was really surprised that Clarissa's still here,' said Ross. 'She walked away from the murder team because she couldn't handle it. And now Frank is in trouble. Now—'

'Well, why are you still here then?' said Hope. 'You've got Angus to think about as well as the little guy.'

'Well, why are you here?' said Ross suddenly. 'You've got

John. You've got Junior in there.'

'Because I can't walk away. These people messed us about. They've messed Seoras about. They've killed people. We're the police. We're the ones here to enforce the law. To bring it to the attention of judges. These people have taken our roles. These people say that they will decide who deserves what and then bring about that justice,' said Hope. 'It's important. It's very important. They're attacking the very thing we are. I can't stand by.'

'I guess so,' said Ross. He felt his phone vibrate and picked it up. He saw a text from Tanya. Jim was on his way down the stairs.

'Uh-oh, better look lively,' said Ross. 'He's on his way down.'

Ross sat with Hope until he saw Jim walk past the canteen. The man had his coat on and was going outside. Ross excused himself politely and then stepped outside through the rear doors of the Inverness station. He was expecting Jim to be walking towards his car, but he didn't. Instead, he turned and took the path at the side of the building out onto the road by the hospital, and then down towards the islands on the River Ness.

It was like a forced hike. Ross kept the distance. It was hard tracking someone who knew you, and Ross was still in his suit and his tie. Rather than cross the river, Ross walked down the side as Jim took to the islands in the middle. Ross watched him walk along before he took the envelope out.

There was a glance left and right by Jim and he dropped the envelope. Without looking at it, he turned and walked away. Suddenly, a man on a bicycle shot past, reached down, grabbed the envelope and was gone.

Jim continued his walk and crossed back on the bridge to

CHAPTER 20

the side Ross was on, forcing Ross to hide behind a parked car. He tailed Jim all the way back to the station.

Ross got the okay from Tanya that Jim was inside his office and went back to his own desk. He sat thinking about what he'd seen. An envelope arrives, and an envelope goes. Ross was uneasy, very uneasy. He placed a call to Clarissa who was clearly driving. Ross reckoned she had the hands-free set on, for he could hear the noise of the cars down in Glasgow.

'Als, what have you got for me? Pats and I are nearly here.'

'I followed the ACC to a warehouse. He got delivered an envelope by a blonde-haired woman. He then took that envelope back here to the station. The ACC then went out again to the islands on the River Ness. There, he dropped the envelope, and it was picked up by a man on a bicycle. The ACC then came back to the station.'

'You what?' said Clarissa. 'He had an envelope passed. You've just seen him taking information.'

'You don't know what information that is,' said a voice on the phone.

'Pats, get a grip,' said Clarissa. 'That's as suspicious as you can get. Phone Macleod. Tell him everything. Als, you've just seen something that could break this case wide open. I mean, who'd have thought it? That's crazy. We're going to go in and talk to the Chief Constable, anyway. But that's just madness. Get Macleod to look into it. Macleod can have a word with him, see what's going on. But we can't answer what he's doing with that envelope, dropping it for collection. Well then, I say he's guilty. In the meantime, keep tailing him. Wherever he goes, you keep on him, all right, Als?'

'I will do,' said Ross, and closed down the call. He was going to call Macleod, but he thought it would be better if he paid a visit. He climbed up the stairs. Ross wondered why he felt nervous. Was it just the idea of it? Was he struggling with the thought that one of these revered people higher up, people he held in high regard, were selling on information?

Ross negotiated Tanya before knocking on Macleod's door, and after a 'come in,' he approached Macleod's desk. The gaffer was smiling, but Ross had a frown on his face that showed worry.

'Sit down, Ross.'

'Thank you, sir.' Ross sat down. 'This is difficult to say,' Ross began.

'It's you and me. Just say it.'

'I've been following the ACC.'

'Jim! Yes, you were meant to. That's good. What of it?'

'I tailed him to a warehouse today. He was inside and a blonde-haired woman approached. Went inside. She disappeared two minutes later. A few minutes later, the ACC came out, and he was holding an envelope.'

'Really?' said Macleod.

'He then came back to the station. After being in the station for an hour, he then went out to the islands on the River Ness. He dropped the envelope, and it was picked up by a man on a bike. I don't know where that man is.'

'Well done, Ross,' said Macleod. Ross could tell that Macleod was livid inside, but he was holding it in.

'Do I need to talk to the Assistant Chief Constable?' asked Ross.

'No,' said Macleod. 'Right line of attack; wrong person to do it. I will speak to him.'

'Do you want me here when you do?'

'No. No, I don't. I think that would only disturb you even

CHAPTER 20

more, Ross.'

'I think you could be right, sir.'

Ross thanked Macleod, who left the room. As he descended the stairs back to his office, he could feel his body shaking. He could not believe they could be betrayed by an Assistant Chief Constable.

Chapter 21

'Smarten your cravat up,' said Clarissa. Patterson looked over at her with a frown. 'Pats, I'm doing this for you, okay? This is the Chief Constable. We're down in amongst the people who really matter in this police force, okay? So, you need to look the part.'

Patterson stared at Clarissa. She was once again in her tartan shawl with her tartan trews underneath. She looked like some wild woman. And yet, she walked around like she was dignified, with an air of grace about her. She was insane.

'Just follow my lead, Pats, okay?'

'Okay,' said the put-upon Patterson.

Patterson followed Clarissa inside the main station and through up to the upper floors where they were greeted by a woman in her late fifties. She had long blonde hair, and smartly done make-up. Not too much, but enough so that it showed. For her age, she seemed to look well and certainly had a no-nonsense attitude about her.

'Detective Inspector Clarissa Urquhart, to see the Chief Constable.'

The secretary looked up and down at her and then over towards Patterson.

CHAPTER 21

'Constable Eric Patterson, I'm with the inspector.' Patterson almost swallowed as the woman looked at him. Her eyes seemed to say, 'Why are you here?' Clarissa, however, didn't seem to be bothered by this. And when the woman went to the phone to check if the chief constable was ready to see them, Clarissa swung around the outer office, checking photographs on the wall as if she was at some sort of arts festival.

'Look at this one, Pats,' she said. 'My, my. That's an old one. Look at the number of men. It's back when they didn't have us women sorting them out.'

Patterson shook his head. He needed to focus here. How did you interview a Chief Constable? How did you ask him if he was dropping the ball? *But then again*, thought Patterson, *maybe that's why Clarissa was sent to do this*.

Clarissa didn't give a hoot. She didn't care who she was talking to. She thought she deserved to be there wherever she was. Frank had also been attacked. Patterson understood why she was the Rottweiler. She would keep going. She wouldn't care what your rank or status was and in truth, right now, she seemed to be in her element.

'The Chief Constable will see you now,' said the secretary and walked out from behind her desk to lead the pair of them to the door on the far side of the office. She rapped on it, opened, and announced their presence, before asking if tea and coffee would be required. The Chief Constable looked at Clarissa and gave a shake of the head.

'I'd rather we weren't disturbed,' said Clarissa. Patterson looked over at the Chief Constable, who clearly thought that this should have been his line. The secretary also looked to the Chief Constable who gave a nod, and she then closed the door behind her.

'Won't you sit down?' said the Chief Constable and Clarissa grabbed the nearest seat to his desk. Patterson advised he would prefer to stand.

'What is it, then, I can do for you?' asked the Chief Constable. 'You've come all the way down from Inverness, and what, a phone call won't do?'

'Regarding the recent situation,' said Clarissa, 'the Revenge group has suffered a major setback. By Loch Lee, they were led into a trap. The information about that meeting and where it was happening, we believe, came from inside the force. We've gone through everyone. We are checking everyone without prejudice. And with that in mind, I would like to ask you what you did with the information received from the Assistant Chief Constable.'

'You think I passed it on?' said the Chief Constable. His face was reddening, and Patterson wondered if he was going to get aggressive. Clarissa, in fairness, hadn't said the man had passed it on. She had said that everyone was being checked, everyone was being looked at, but neither had she softened the blow that much.

'This is quite ridiculous,' said the Chief Constable after a moment.

'Is it?' asked Clarissa. 'Is it really? The Forseti group has been a pain for a long time. The idea someone would prompt the Revenge group to take action on some of their best people is understandable if not acceptable. The Forseti group is replacing us. They're stepping in and doing our job. Taking power away from us. They're an offence to every decent police officer. Why wouldn't someone help take them out? My husband has been targeted. I wouldn't mind seeing a lot of their heads up on a spike somewhere.'

CHAPTER 21

Patterson closed his eyes. She was always so melodramatic. Up on a spike somewhere. Not just arrested. And then he thought about it. Actually, if she'd have been there, never mind Anna Hunt despatching the hitman, Clarissa would have done it with her bare hands. Or at least tried to.

'It hasn't come out of this office. I got an update from the ACC. When I got that update, I made a note of it, but it didn't go anywhere. The information's not left this office. Now, it's more common knowledge but at that time, it hadn't gone from here. It was held within this office.'

'Do you have any doubts about any of your Assistant Chief Constables?' asked Clarissa.

'No. And anyway, the only one that's been involved with this case has been Jim. None of the others have taken part in it. None of the others have information about it. And I've absolutely no doubt about any of them.'

'So,' said Clarissa, 'you're telling me you received the information and the information didn't go anywhere?'

'It has since. I have briefed the ACCs on what happened because with the Service being involved—with the hushing up and the uniform sections of Glasgow then investigating a bus crash that didn't actually happen—it made sense for them to be aware and not ask pointless questions. But that information came out long after the incident. The Revenge group had been attacked at least the day before, if not two, by the time the ACCs got the information.'

'And just to reiterate,' said Clarissa, 'the information didn't leave this office. You didn't take it home on a laptop, you didn't—'

'I am capable of understanding where information goes, and when it's important, how to hang on to it,' said the Chief

Constable. 'Frankly, I don't like that tone.'

'And frankly, I don't like the situation I'm in,' said Clarissa, 'where I've got a mole or somebody in this police force when I'm dealing with people who will cut us dead in an instant.'

She was up on her feet now, and Patterson watched. There was restraint there, but if you didn't know Clarissa, you wouldn't have seen it. If this had been an ordinary person, if this had been a lower-ranked officer, she might have been round the table at him, trying to force out the information she wanted. But instead, for now, she was holding her ground.

'Like I said, the information never left this office.'

'Thank you,' said Clarissa. 'We'll advise you when we find out where it went and who from.'

'Do that,' said the Chief Constable. 'And tell Macleod that if you're going to come down with accusations like that, I'd appreciate it if a more senior officer was here to speak their mind.'

'I think you'll find that DCI Macleod's a rather busy man,' said Clarissa. 'So he sent someone to get the truth.'

Patterson nearly gasped at that one. But she swung round quickly, the tartan shawl flapping behind her, and made for the door. She had it open before Patterson had moved, and Clarissa flicked her head round.

'Come on, Pats, I think we got what we needed.'

Patterson gave a brief thank you to the Chief Constable but the man's face was raging. He followed Clarissa out, out to the car where they sat for a moment.

'Well, he might be lying,' said Clarissa. 'I can't tell. No wiser than when we went in.'

'Maybe not the best approach,' said Patterson.

'If you're going to criticise the way I'm running things, you

CHAPTER 21

can get out of this car now. All right, Pats? You're here to support me. I don't need any of that at the moment.'

Patterson ignored her and then said, 'Do you realise something? He said that the information never left his office.'

'Yes, I heard him,' said Clarissa.

'Never left his office,' said Patterson. 'He didn't say, "I told no one."'

'What do you mean?' asked Clarissa, suddenly interested.

'He said it never left his office. What's his office? If the information came to you personally, you would say "I told no one." But if it's never left his office, that means people within what he describes as his office, knew.'

'Well, there's only him there, and his secretary.'

'Why would his secretary know?' asked Patterson.

'You're right, Pats. You're not just a cravat in a suit.' Patterson gave her a glare for that one. 'But you're on it, Pats. Right, I'm going to go back up there to have a word with that secretary.'

Clarissa was nearly out of the seat of the car when Patterson reached over and grabbed her wrist.

'Can I suggest a different course of action?' he said politely, but firmly.

'What?' asked Clarissa.

'One,' said Patterson, 'you don't go back into that building. You've wound them up. If he's spoken to his secretary, she'll be on the defensive from you.'

'I guess that's fair,' said Clarissa.

'Two, I go up. I go up and decide I need to make a phone call to somewhere else. Just to use her phone. And then get to talk to her. Get some information.'

'Good idea,' said Clarissa.

'Right,' said Patterson, 'I'll go.'

He stepped out of the car, and closed the door behind him. Clarissa called after him. 'What do you want from the bakery?'

'What?' said Patterson.

'Pats, what do you want from the bakery? I'll get you a coffee as well.'

'Why are you going off for a coffee?' said Patterson. 'We're in the middle of work.'

'It will not look sensible if I'm sitting here in the car while you go back up. Okay? Let's say that something's annoyed me, so I'm going off to get some buns or whatever. I'm not sitting here waiting around for you. It doesn't really fit me, does it?'

Patterson had to concede. 'So what do you want?' asked Clarissa.

'Surprise me,' said Patterson.

'Like a cream pie to the face,' said Clarissa. She started the car and drove off, leaving Patterson to walk back into the station. He made his way up to the top floor and caught the secretary.

'Sorry to bother you,' he said. 'I was meant to take down the timings of our meeting. She's very particular about that, the boss. You can see what she's like.'

'Oh, right,' said the secretary. 'I'll have it in here because he'll have his notes of having met with you. Let me just get that for you.'

'So you take notes of all his meetings, do you?'

'I take down whatever the Chief Constable wants.'

'Right. Well, thank you for those,' said Patterson, looking down. He saw the woman had gone into a secure file, for she made sure Patterson wasn't looking at the screen whenever she typed in what he thought was a password.

'Would it be okay to use your phone,' said Patterson. 'My phone's gone dead, and I really could do with talking to

CHAPTER 21

someone up at the station. Back at Inverness.'

'Sure,' she said, and pointed over to a phone at the far end of her desk. 'Use that one. Normal procedures for an outside line.'

'Cheers,' said Patterson. He placed a call to Hope, who picked it up. 'Hi there,' Patterson said. 'I'm looking into the portfolio. I'm just wondering if you've looked into it. I'd suggest you take a good look.'

On the other end of the phone, Hope gave a nod to herself. 'I will do. Just hold the line.' She put the phone down on her desk and went back to looking at some paperwork. Meanwhile, Patterson stood politely at the desk of the Chief Constable's assistant.

'She's gone off to get some stuff,' said Patterson. 'How long have you worked for him?'

'Oh, it's been twenty years, at least,' said the secretary. 'Started when he was a Chief Inspector. He's done well for himself.'

'Oh, he has that. I mean, to be up with the top, but must be a lot of pressure.'

'Oh, it is. It is a lot. He relies on me.'

'You get a lot of information going back and forward, I imagine,' said Patterson. 'It's awkward, isn't it? You have to know who to trust. You have to have someone you can bond with. I guess after twenty years, the two of you must be pretty tight as a team.'

'I would say that.'

'It's good that he trusts you, though,' said Patterson. 'I have a hell of a time with her. You see what she's like. She's just boom, boom, boom. Is he like that? You ever get fed up with him?'

'No. I say we work well together. He trusts me with a lot. He knows I can handle his information. But you have to guard him, too, you know.'

'Ward off anyone coming in. You do a good job of that,' said Patterson. 'An excellent job. You always been in Glasgow?'

'Well, he's never moved out,' said the secretary. 'I was born and bred, too. Never really wanted to go anywhere else.'

'Good job, then. You ever find the pressure gets to you? I know it does in my job.'

'No, we don't have the pressure the same as you guys,' said the secretary.

'Yes, but you're handling top-level stuff. I mean, there're situations, things like that, that you must . . . well, you must know, even just from keeping notes. It's a trouble, isn't it? Once you've read something, you can't sort of hide it. You have to be—'

'You have to be very confidential,' she said. 'He relies on me for that. He has done for twenty years. Never let him down, though.'

'Right,' said Patterson. 'Oh,' he said, 'you've got it.' He was back talking on the phone again. 'That's good,' he said. 'Thank you for that. We'll see you shortly.'

Patterson's voice was loud as he signed off. Up in Inverness, Hope could hear him speaking again and put the phone down.

He turned to the secretary. 'Thank you for that. I'd better get going before she loses it. She's gone off anyway. She said she had to go to the bakery or something. That's the thing. You'd think she could wait for five minutes while I ran up and did this, but she's pissed at me because I didn't get it at the time. You've saved my bacon, though. You really have,' said Patterson. 'Thank you.'

CHAPTER 21

He disappeared down the stairs, waving a hand at the woman. But as he descended, he realised he was right. The information had gone into the office. They weren't just looking at the Chief Constable here. They were looking at his secretary as well. The Chief Constable never mentioned that. He'd referred to it implicitly. It was in his office. But he never said about her. He never looked to question her. They would have to. After all, they had to treat everybody without prejudice. She had the information. They would need to think and examine to see if she used it.

Chapter 22

'Tanya, can you ask the Assistant Chief Constable to come see me in my office?'

Macleod sat back in his chair. This was going to be the hardest conversation he'd had in a long time, and he needed to be thorough, but also in control. No doubt this would get heated. He looked around his office. Sitting on the chair in front of his desk was Hope. She looked agitated, and he didn't blame her. Ross was standing uncomfortably over by the wall, and then sitting almost in shadow was Kirsten.

She didn't look nervous at all. She looked focused and determined. Macleod wondered how many people she had put under pressure when she was working for the Service. In some ways, he didn't want to know. He was used to operating within the confines of an interview room. That wasn't what he wanted here. He wanted the pressure you feel in a foreign environment.

Jim would understand an interview room. He knew what you could and couldn't ask. He knew what would be admissible and what wasn't. But this wasn't about evidence. This was about getting to the top man in the Forseti group which meant that they had to go the roundabout route, by finding who had

CHAPTER 22

leaked to the Revenge group. Only then would they work out how that person had been played by the Forseti group—how they had known there was already a mole for the Revenge group.

There was a knock on the door. Macleod told the knocker to 'come in' and Tanya opened the door, introducing the Assistant Chief Constable. Macleod held a hand open, showing the second chair in front of his desk for Jim. Tanya asked would they be requiring coffee. Macleod politely said no, there wouldn't be any need on this occasion. He also told Tanya there was to be no chance of a disruption to this meeting. Tanya nodded and closed the door.

Jim looked around the room until he stopped, focusing on Kirsten in the corner.

'What's this then? You didn't say we were meeting with others. You didn't say there was—'

'Just take the seat, Jim,' said Macleod.

Jim slowly sat down, and Macleod looked over at Ross. 'DS Ross, would you explain what you saw?'

'Yes, sir,' said Ross. 'I was tailing the Assistant Chief Constable—'

'You were what?' cried Jim.

'I was tailing you, sir. Under the instruction of DI Clarissa Urquhart.'

'Who was operating under my direct instruction,' said Macleod. 'Carry on, Ross.'

'Very good, sir. I was tailing the Assistant Chief Constable. He went to an abandoned warehouse on an estate on the edge of Inverness. There, he entered the warehouse. Shortly afterwards a blonde-haired woman arrived, entered the building, came out two minutes later, and disappeared. I continued to watch the building and the Assistant Chief Constable emerged with an envelope that he then tucked away.

'He came back here to the station, spent an hour up in his office and then went out to the islands on the River Ness. He didn't take his car; he walked there. Once on the island, he took out the envelope. He dropped it, and a man on a bicycle sped past, grabbed it off the ground, and disappeared. The Assistant Chief Constable then returned here to the station.'

'At any time did he interact with anyone else with that envelope?' asked Macleod.

'Not that I am aware of, sir, but obviously once he's gone inside his office, I wasn't watching him. He was in his own private quarters.'

'Well done, Ross. Thank you.' Macleod turned and looked at Jim. 'I'd like you to explain what's going on,' he said.

'You haul me down in front of these people. They're not at my level, Macleod,' said Jim. 'You should have another ACC sat with you. You should have somebody else of a higher rank. You have a Detective Inspector, a DS and God only knows what position she holds.' Jim pointed over at Kirsten.

'I'm here,' said Macleod. 'I'm the DCI involved in this investigation. It is my investigation, and it has been compromised by a leak within the force. I am asking you to account for suspicious activities.'

'You put a tail on me. Do you not trust me?'

'I've trusted no one with this. I have gone through my entire team. Trust me, I have been investigated. Not because I had doubts about myself, but because you never know when you can give something away by accident. So, we monitored everyone. And lo-and-behold, you turned up with a suspicious package. An envelope. An envelope you then dropped for

CHAPTER 22

someone else.'

'I can't tell you about that.'

'That sounds remarkably convenient,' said Hope.

'You remember your place, Detective Inspector. This is your Assistant Chief Constable you're talking to.'

'She's talking to somebody who's displaying rather suspicious activity,' said Kirsten.

'You don't get to talk,' said Jim, and turned to Macleod. 'I can't talk about this. You push this, you could jeopardise everything.'

'That's not good enough,' said Macleod. 'That's a cover.'

'I can't talk about this. I'm doing this for a reason.'

'And so am I,' said Macleod. 'At the moment, I am investigating possible collusion that caused the deaths of many people. I am not backing down on this one, Jim. You need to give me an answer. You tell me to clear the room and speak to me, fine. I'll do it. But at the moment you're not giving me an answer.'

'No,' said Jim. 'No, no, it doesn't work like that. I'm the ACC. I have certain things that you cannot know about. You cannot know about this.' He stood up. 'This meeting is over. Do not speak of it. Do not bring it up again.' Jim turned to march to the door.

Before he got there, Kirsten stepped in front of him. Jim was taller than her, but he was clearly intimidated by Kirsten. She may have been small, only about five foot four, but she was trim. Kirsten looked like she could handle herself.

'You will sit down, and you will answer whatever questions DCI Macleod asks of you,' said Kirsten. 'Because if you don't, I will call in Anna Hunt. I will bring the Service into this.'

'You tell her to stand down,' Jim said to Macleod. 'You tell her to get out of my way.'

'I don't tell her what to do. I could ask her, but I think her being in the way is what I want at the moment,' said Macleod.

'This is ridiculous. This is bloody ridiculous,' said Jim. He put a hand on Kirsten's shoulder to move her out of the way, but found his arm whipped up behind his back. He was then driven all the way back to his seat and plonked in it. Kirsten stood right beside him.

'That's assault,' said Jim.

'Trust me,' said Kirsten. 'That was a gentle encouragement to go back to your seat. Now answer the man.'

Jim looked anxious. Sweat was forming on his brow.

'If it's something to do with the force,' said Macleod, 'if it's genuine, Jim, none of it will go beyond any of us. I trust these three people with my life. But, if it's genuine and you hold on to this, Anna Hunt will find out about it. Better to have it with us in the force than outside, I would suggest. Because either way, we're finding out what this is.'

Jim looked this way and that. He looked up at Kirsten. She was still glaring at him.

'I went to pick up that envelope on instruction from a higher-up source within the force.'

'What was in it, then?' asked Hope.

'I don't know. It went to the source. It goes up above me. All I'm doing is picking up.'

'Why you?' asked Macleod. 'I mean, why you?'

Jim was looking around him now. He was ragged.

'I don't believe you,' said Hope. 'I truly don't. It was the woman that delivered the envelope.'

Jim stopped for a moment. 'No one delivered the envelope,' he said.

'What do you mean?' asked Macleod. 'Ross saw her. She

CHAPTER 22

delivered the envelope.'

'What woman?' In his outrage at the idea of Ross tailing him, Jim had clearly missed the detail on the woman in Ross's report. 'My instructions from my contact higher up was that I should go there. An envelope would be waiting inside. I had to go through two corridors and into a room. I was to pick up the envelope, but however, I was to wait inside for five minutes before exiting.'

Macleod looked over at Ross.

'He was indeed about five minutes.'

'And you never saw a woman?' asked Macleod.

'No,' said Jim. Kirsten glared at him.

'Ross?'

'Yes, sir.'

'Was it possible that the Assistant Chief Constable didn't see the woman?'

'He went inside the building. She entered the building a minute or two later. She was in quickly, then back out. I can't say for definite that they made contact within. I can't say what the inside of that building looked like as I didn't go in. So, he could have done as he said. They may not have met. I certainly can't prove that they did.'

Macleod stood up for a moment. He walked to the window and then he looked back before he stared out the window again. He looked over at Kirsten. 'Is he lying?' he asked her.

'I don't believe so,' she said.

'I don't believe so either,' said Macleod. 'Are you thinking what I'm thinking?'

'A bluff,' said Kirsten.

'A bluff?' said Hope. 'What do you mean, a bluff?'

'Jim, I think you've been played,' said Macleod. 'I can't prove

187

it yet but you're going to tell me exactly who that envelope is for.'

'I can't do that. They rely on me. They rely on me to do this because they wouldn't trust these things to someone at lower levels. You would never—'

'The chief constable,' said Macleod.

Jim's face fell. Kirsten turned and looked at Macleod, smiling. 'Yes,' she said, 'that was genuine.'

'It is the Chief Constable,' said Jim. 'That does not leave this room. From time to time, he asks me to pick stuff up for him. He gets information sometimes from sources he doesn't like to meet. Sometimes they're sources he doesn't wholly trust. Usually, the information is left like this, in an envelope somewhere. I'll drop it on, and he'll get somebody else to pick it up for him.'

'It's all rather elaborate,' said Macleod.

'You could just tell him,' said Ross. 'You could tell him, sir, when you're with him. You have plenty of meetings with him.'

'This sort of information, this sort of knowledge, isn't coming from sources you can quote in an investigation.'

'That makes sense,' said Kirsten.

'It all begins to make sense to me,' said Macleod.

'Really?' said Hope. 'All I know at the moment is that Jim here works for our Chief Constable. If what he says is true, I don't see the problem with it. He's working on the quiet to give the Chief Constable information from sources the Chief can't meet.'

'There's nothing wrong with that,' said Macleod. 'What bothers me now is that it's been made out that Jim is the problem. Ross tailed him. They must have known we would look at everybody. They must have known they'd be tailed.

CHAPTER 22

The Chief Constable has a way of getting Jim to go somewhere in the quiet that nobody else knows about. He's been tailed and been found out. Suddenly, this other woman appears. Because if Jim just picked up the envelope, it would make a lot more sense. Instead, this woman comes in. Jim will deny all knowledge of her. They're thinking that we'll then believe he's a liar. But he's not. Jim has told the truth. Completely. Whoever it is, doesn't understand that he's trusted us.'

'It's a bluff,' said Kirsten, 'to throw confusion, to make you doubt each other. It's a bluff to establish this idea that Jim's at the heart of this message being passed on. A bluff that can only be purported because they needed to cover something else. They needed us to think it came from us. The instruction, the information, that the meeting of the Forseti group was passed on to the Revenge group by us. They had to have us believe that so they could cover up something else. A different connection.'

'To what purpose?' asked Hope.

'We need to talk to the Chief Constable again,' said Macleod. 'Somebody knew how Jim operated and set him up. The people who knew how that worked, as far as we know, are Jim and the Chief Constable. Anyone else you know of, Jim?'

'No,' said Jim. 'It was between us.'

'That remains to be seen,' said Macleod. 'They keep playing us. They played us this time. But I think I'm beginning to see the game.'

Chapter 23

Macleod received a call from Clarissa advising how her meeting with the Chief Constable had gone. She also voiced Patterson's ideas about where information within the office went which grabbed Macleod's attention immediately. Jim was still in his office along with Kirsten, Hope and Ross, and Macleod decided that now was the time. He couldn't just call the Chief Constable and demand to talk to him. But Jim could. Jim could get there.

The man had calmed down somewhat, but he still looked agitated and annoyed. Inside, he must have been worried. He'd been played. But then Macleod thought, what was new about that? They'd been getting played for the last while.

Macleod asked Clarissa to go to the Chief Constable's office, advising she'd be let in. He suggested Patterson should maybe wait outside, and Clarissa agreed.

'Keep this call on speakerphone,' Macleod said to Jim, 'so we can all hear.'

He placed the call and asked to get through to the Chief Constable and then let Jim take the phone call. The Chief Constable's secretary asked if it was important and Jim said yes. He was put through immediately.

CHAPTER 23

'Jim, what's the matter?'

'Angus, we've got a problem.'

'What do you mean, "we've got a problem?"'

'I'm in the office of Detective Chief Inspector Macleod. We've been getting played.'

'What?' said Angus.

'We've been getting played. I went to pick up a package for you. An envelope.'

'No, you didn't. I haven't asked for any envelope to be picked up. It's been a while since I needed you for that.'

'You did. I got a call on my phone, the special phone, asking me to pick it up.'

'I can't confirm that,' said Macleod on the speakerphone. 'But Detective Sergeant Ross followed the Assistant Chief Constable and saw him pick up an envelope from an abandoned warehouse. There was also a lady who arrived and then disappeared.'

'Why do they know about the envelopes? Why do they know what you're doing for me?' asked Angus. 'Jim, this was classified. You knew this was top secret, not to talk about this. You've told them. Seriously, you—'

'We're beyond that,' said Jim. 'Well beyond that.'

'I don't see how we are.'

'Chief Constable,' said Macleod. 'We are beyond that. We are tracing the leak to the Revenge group. Only I'm not so sure there is a leak at the moment. I need you to tell me about the packages you and Jim are involved in. The ones you ask him to pick up.'

'You do not need to know about those,' said Angus.

'I'm afraid that genie's out of the bottle,' said Macleod. 'I know about them. What I need to know is when you last gave

Jim an instruction.'

'I haven't given Jim an instruction to pick anything up in months. I speak very privately to him. It's meant to be done on a basis where nobody finds out. Bloody hell, Jim. You can't do this. This compromises things.'

'You have been compromised anyway,' said Macleod. 'What sort of information goes into these packages?'

'What do you mean, what sort of information? I will not tell you what sort of information it is.'

'I told them,' said Jim, 'it's things they can't know about, coming from sources that you can't be directly linked to. It's your quiet line in. There's nothing wrong with it. They know that.'

'But I didn't give Jim an instruction. He hasn't had to pick anything up, not in a couple of months.'

'I regret to inform you,' said Macleod, 'that he went, picked up an envelope, came back, and dropped it off on the River Ness Islands.'

'Which warehouse was it, Jim?' asked Angus.

'Number three.'

'So you have certain places?' asked Macleod. 'Certain fixed places.'

'Yes,' said Angus.

'So who would know that? Who holds your secret information?'

'I told your inspector when she was here.'

'And she's here right now,' said Clarissa.

'How did you get in?' said Angus.

'You need to lock your door if you don't want me to come in,' said Clarissa. 'I'm in place, Seoras.'

Macleod could hear a slight kerfuffle on the other end of the

CHAPTER 23

phone.

'The Chief Constable thought I shouldn't be in the room, but I'm still here,' said Clarissa. 'He's sitting down now to answer some questions.'

Macleod gave a wry smile. 'Where does the information in your office go?'

'What information?' said Angus.

'The stuff nobody else is meant to know. Who holds it? Who sees it?'

'It's for me. It remains within my office.'

'When you say your office,' asked Macleod, 'is your office just you? Is your secretary part of your office?'

'Laura? Laura will see some of it. She files it away. She keeps it secret. It's all securely locked within either files or on computer systems. People can't get it. They can't hack in.'

'But she has access,' said Macleod.

'She doesn't read it. She files it away for me. If she has to type up, she has to type up. It's not a problem. Twenty years. It's not been a problem.'

'What's her name?' asked Macleod.

'Laura Kinley. You don't need to ask me that. You could look that up in the records. She's an employee. She's been vetted.'

'How did you know her? Where did you find her?' asked Macleod.

'It was back when I worked as a detective inspector, one of the Glasgow stations. She applied for work. We needed someone, just a secretary at the time. She's now more my PA. But Laura Kinley came in. She was, what, about thirty years old then. Met her at a Christmas do. Moved her over to our team, because we had the post that came up. She's been with us ever since.

'Laura's solid. She wouldn't betray anyone. Laura's helped in many ways. You're barking up the wrong tree here, Macleod. Laura's not like that. She's held too many secrets. They haven't gone out.'

Macleod pressed the intercom button and asked for Tanya to come in.

'Tanya, with your HR connections, get me Laura Kinley's file. I want to know everything about her. Everything.'

'Of course,' said Tanya, and brusquely left the room.

'You won't find anything. I'll tell you now, you'll find nothing. She's solid. A good egg.'

'There's a bad egg somewhere,' said Macleod, 'and I'm going to find it.'

'But why would she tell them? Why? What could she hope to gain?' said Angus.

'I don't know. I really don't know,' said Macleod. 'You see, she told them things. But she didn't tell them about the Forseti meeting, about Loch Lee. That's not what she told them about.'

'What are you on about, man?' said Angus.

'We think there's a leak from the force, one that sent the Revenge group to Loch Lee. But the Forseti group knew they were coming. The Forseti group set us up to pass that information on. I believe they set up your secretary. But not to get the Revenge group there.'

Inside the Chief Constable's office, Clarissa was standing in front of the door, making sure the man couldn't leave it. He was sitting in his chair with a bit of room between him and her now. She could sense he was glad of that.

'We got played,' said Macleod, 'but we got really played. Played to a point you don't even understand.'

'What do you mean?' cried the Chief Constable.

CHAPTER 23

'We were not the ones who passed on the message,' said Macleod.

'How? Where else did they learn it from?'

'This is their story. Every time. Bluff. Double bluff. They want us running around here, searching, looking, because something else is going on.'

'What in the name of all that is good and holy, Macleod, are you on about?' asked Angus.

There was a knock at the office door and by the strength and steadiness of the rap, Macleod knew it was Tanya. He asked her to come in, and she strode over to him, handing him a file. He placed it down on his desk, thanked Tanya, and she left the room while Macleod opened up the file and scanned it.

'It checks out what you're saying,' said Macleod, 'about her being hired.'

'I told you, there's nothing dodgy in this.'

'Nothing dodgy about you,' said Macleod. 'But this is interesting.'

'What?' asked Angus. Macleod could see the rest of the team in his room were looking in as well. Hope had stood up and come over to the file. Macleod was pointing down at a line that said 'maiden name.'

'She used to be Laura Matthews. That was her maiden name. I wonder if she's linked to Simon Matthews, Emma Matthews, all the Matthews.'

'Oh, bloody hell,' said Angus.

'DI Urquhart,' said Macleod. 'Kindly get Mrs Kinley to come in.'

'Will do,' said Clarissa. She came back two minutes later. 'It appears Miss Kinley has left the office. I think the Chief Constable is requiring some time alone.'

'I didn't know anything about that side of her. I didn't—'

'You trusted her,' said Macleod. 'You trusted her with things you were trusting next to no one else with. Why? She was just a secretary, a PA? You never really knew where she came from?' he asked.

'But she . . . she was . . . she kept . . .'

'She did what?' asked Macleod.

'She kept it quiet when I had the affair.'

'The one with her?' asked Macleod.

'Well, that too.'

'That too?' blurted Clarissa. 'What on earth?'

'Easy, Inspector Urquhart,' said Macleod. 'Which affair? What affairs?' asked Macleod.

'I had an affair, and she covered it up for me. I also slept with her.'

Macleod looked up and saw Jim's face. His jaw had dropped. He was shaking his head in disbelief.

'And she's gone,' said Jim.

* * *

Laura Kinley had heard most of the conversation. She often listened in to what the Chief Constable was saying, and she realised the number was up. Laura had grabbed her things and was walking down to her car as if nothing was wrong. She'd gone by her locker to clear it out as well and had planned to walk nimbly to the car and just drive off. She'd disappear, because she knew now someone would come. They had said that when it came, they would help her. They would relocate her and her husband. They would make it okay.

She was going to call that favour in. She walked past the

CHAPTER 23

entrance doors, then through the small side door that led out to the car park. Once there, she glanced around. Nobody. That was fine.

Laura walked over to the car, opened the door, and got inside. She reached for a key and then thought of something. She'd locked the car this morning, hadn't she? Hadn't she? She reached down into her pocket. That was the wrong key that she'd grabbed. That was a house key. Where was the car key? She looked inside her handbag. There was a spare key there. She always carried the spare in the handbag and the actual one on her. The one she carried on her was gone.

She looked out of the window. Then she looked in the rearview mirror. Rising from the back seat was a man with a smart cravat around his neck.

'I introduced myself before, but it's DC Patterson. And where are you going?' he asked.

'Just going home,' she said. 'How did you—'

'An old trick,' said Patterson. 'It's not difficult when you engage people, talk to them. I have a feeling some people want to talk to you, upstairs, and that's where we're going to go. Don't try anything daft, please. And let's not make a fuss on the way up. Keep this nice and quiet. Probably safer for you, too. If whoever you work for gets wind that you're in trouble, they might cut their losses completely. Termination, I would guess. I take it you have a real husband? That ring isn't fake.'

Patterson could see the tears in Laura's eyes. She was trembling.

Chapter 24

Clarissa stood at one side of the office and noticed that the Chief Constable couldn't look at her. She was enjoying this, although she'd not admit to it, at least not to anybody but herself. Clarissa had a thing against the upper echelons of the Police. She'd never risen high enough, not for her abilities, not until Macleod had taken an interest.

Yes, she was gruff; she knew that. Of course, she was gruff. She was rude, and probably arrogant with it too. But she got the job done, and she got it done well. She struck fear into the heart of criminals. That was part of it. Wasn't that how it worked?

There came a knock on the office door, and it was pushed open. Laura McKinley walked in, and behind her was Patterson.

'Good lad, Pats,' said Clarissa. 'That's Laura here now, Seoras,' she said over to the speakerphone. She saw the Chief Constable turn and stare at Laura. The woman gave a shrug of the shoulders, but she didn't sit beside him. She kept herself almost as far away as possible. The Chief Constable was angry, raging, and as soon as Laura sat down in the chair, distanced from him, he stood up and walked towards her.

CHAPTER 24

'You bitch!' he shouted. 'Did it mean nothing? All these years, it meant nothing to you! All these years you just strung me along.'

Clarissa stepped in between the two of them, but the chief constable tried to push past.

'Look at yourself!' shouted Laura. 'Hardest thing I ever did was get on top of that body of yours. That was sacrifice!'

Clarissa did her best not to burst out laughing. Instead, she put on an intense face and yelled at the Chief Constable to sit down.

'Pats, you sit on him, I'll sit on her. Okay. Seoras, do you want to start with these questions or am I just going to be sitting here holding on to people for the rest of the day?'

'I didn't realise you were in a hurry,' said Macleod from the other end. 'Good afternoon, Mrs McKinley,' said Macleod. 'I realise you may be in a bit of shock at the moment at being found out. However, it will go much better for you if you actually answer our questions. Who first got you into the office of the Chief Constable?'

The woman started to mumble, but Macleod couldn't hear and Clarissa, aware of it, told them to hang on a moment. She took the woman round to sit in the Chief Constable's chair beside his phone and got Patterson to move him to the far end of the office. Once there, Clarissa urged her with a simple tap on the back to begin speaking.

'It's been years,' she said. 'McIntosh. After his father was killed, he approached me, asked me what we could do. Asked me to go into the police force, find out if anyone in the police force was part of the group who had brought down his father. But I had to go in quietly, so I started off as a secretary. And then, Angus asked me to come across and work for his team as a secretary. And I stayed with him because he was a climber. He was on the way up. And McIntosh said it would be worth it.'

'When you say McIntosh,' asked Macleod, 'do you mean the senior son?'

'Well, he's the McIntosh, isn't he? Running the family, or at least him and his mother. I've just been feeding them information. Back and forward lines of communication. More to do with anything around Forseti. I haven't given them lots of information on crimes and that. That's not what I'm about. I'm a Matthews, not a McIntosh.'

'So, the McIntoshes have been able to understand all about our investigations, everything we've been doing. Is that how the group was ahead of us? How the group understood our investigations, where we were going?' asked Macleod.

'They thought you could find out more than they could. And they were right. You've narrowed the field. You've got closer to the head of this group than anyone ever has. We'd thank you for it, but you probably wouldn't enjoy it.'

'So on that day, what happened?' asked Macleod.

'The Assistant Chief Constable called with news of the attack. It was hard. There were people there I'd worked with for years. And they were now dead. It was a colossal blow. When it came through, I was brought in by the Chief Constable. We made a note and filed it away; what was happening and what times.'

'And what did you do with the information personally?' asked Macleod. 'Did you pass it on?'

'I did,' she said. 'I got no response, but I sent it on to a mobile that will now be broken up. You won't find the mobile.'

'When did you send it on?'

'Immediately, after I'd found out. I was in the office, I had to

CHAPTER 24

make a note for the Chief Constable, but as soon as I left the office, I messaged it.'

'What time did you make the note?' asked Macleod.

'I don't remember exactly,' said Laura.

'Go into the system,' said Macleod, 'whatever one you have for holding it on the quiet, the secret system you've got, and tell me when you made it.'

Clarissa watched, allowing the woman to access computer terminals. She disappeared into the system, worked files, and then said to Macleod, 'It was twenty-five past the hour.'

'Hang on,' said Macleod. 'They were already on the move. They were already going at that point. In fact, they'd been going for fifteen minutes. They'd left the longhouse, everything. They knew their coordinates. Are you sure about that time?'

'I am sure.'

Back in Inverness, Macleod looked over at Kirsten. She nodded to him. Double bluff. They bluffed. It never came from here.

'That means,' said Macleod, 'that there's a plant in the Revenge group. Somebody had to feed them the information. Somebody had to tell them. They had to get it from somewhere.'

'Who's the leak?' asked Hope.

'It would have to be close,' said Macleod. 'They committed lots of people. They were committed to be in vans with guns. If they got stopped, they'd get hauled in, be in jail. Their organisation could be cut down. So they must have believed they were going at the right time. They must have trusted the source. They must also have been fed a great story.'

'Who,' asked Ross, 'would betray them? These are not people out for money. All the people in the Revenge group were stung.

All the people in the Revenge group were hit with family who had died because of what the Forseti group did. They weren't doing this for money. They're not mercenaries. What would make them do it? What would make them give them up?'

'If it's not money,' said Macleod, 'it has to be something else. It has to be something that you would get by a lot of them disappearing.'

'Her eldest son would lead,' said Hope, looking at Macleod.

'Her eldest son would lead,' said Macleod. 'Absolutely. And if he gets taken out and gets killed and a lot of his lieutenants get killed too, the group's reduced. The McIntosh family, though it's not big—who runs it then? The younger boy. Always kept down.'

'The younger boy!' said Clarissa.

'The younger boy,' said Hope. 'Younger boy could take over. Mother's shrewd, but she's not strong. She won't go out and do anything. She's always favoured the older one.'

'And if he went on the word of the family. On the word of his younger brother. That's why they went. Because they trusted him. They trusted him. The source was good. Trustworthy.'

Macleod grabbed his phone, dialling for Emmett.

'Emmett, we just worked it out. There was no call from here that mattered. The group already knew. The Revenge group were already on their way to the site. Somebody else had told them. Somebody within the group. Somebody within the group betrayed them. Forseti have a link in. And I think it's the youngest one. The youngest McIntosh son.'

'Uh-oh. Say that again,' said Emmett.

'What?'

'Ellen McIntosh just left the house with her youngest son. Just the two of them in a car.'

CHAPTER 24

'What? Do you know where they went?'

'I put Perry and Susan on following her, just in case.'

'Phone them. Tell them they're to stop the pair of them,' bellowed Macleod.

'Stop them?'

'Yes,' said Macleod. 'Her oldest son has just died from bad information coming through, and now she goes out on her own with her son? One of them's not making a return trip,' said Macleod.

'On it,' said Emmett. Emmett closed the call.

* * *

Perry was sitting in the car with Susan, outside what was a rather run-down tenement. In truth, most of the houses were occupied, but none of them looked in particularly good repair. Ellen McIntosh and her youngest son had entered one in the middle of the street. It looked fairly unoccupied, and Perry had wondered why they were even here. However, he was just watching.

Susan picked up a call on her mobile. 'Yes, it's Susan.'

For a moment, she listened to Emmett detailing. Exhaling. And then her face went white.

'What is it?' asked Perry, seeing the change.

'We need to get in there,' said Susan, closing the phone down.

She'd opened the door. Perry was getting out the other side, but he was bemused. 'Why? Why are we getting in like this? They'll see us.'

'One of them isn't coming out. One of them isn't.'

Susan ran up to the door. 'It's locked, Perry. It's closed.' Perry ran up behind her, jumped and thundered into it with his shoulder. He let out a yell.

'Damn it! I shouldn't have done that.'

Susan ran back to the car. She then came back with an axe.

'Bloody hell,' said Perry. Susan told him to step aside, and she started battering in at the lock. It was the work of a few minutes before the door swung open. Perry pushed it, ran round the lower level of the tenement, but there was no one there, and then, followed by Susan, he desperately climbed up the stairs.

'Police!' he shouted. 'It's the police! Stand down!'

A gunshot went off. Perry instinctively ducked, but then he continued on up. He glanced quickly into the first bedroom, but there was no one there. He flung open the door of the bedroom at the front, throwing himself against the wall as he did so, but there was only silence from inside the room. Perry peered in quickly, then back out.

He saw Ellen McIntosh standing with a gun in her hand. He then leaned in to see if the younger McIntosh was there, peering in quickly, realising she wasn't paying him any attention. On the far wall, a man was slumped. High above his head, blood had been spattered all over the wall. Indeed, half his head was probably there. What had remained of him had slid down, lying in a sort of crumpled heap. Perry stepped in gingerly.

'Put the gun down, Ellen,' he said. 'Please put the gun down. I don't want to take action.'

'He was mine. Wee bastard gave his brother up. He gave us up. This. He gave up the whole organisation for what? To run it? To run what? There's nothing left. There's no Revenge group after this. He couldn't do it. And why? Why would he do it? Do you have kids?' she asked, looking at Perry directly.

CHAPTER 24

Perry shook his head. 'No, but put the gun down. Just put the gun down.'

'Then you wouldn't understand.' Before Perry could react, she put the gun under her chin and pulled the trigger.

Susan came racing in but Perry caught her and pushed her back out. 'No! No, no! No! Together, the two of them fell to the ground. Perry buried his face in her shoulder, holding on to her tight. There was nothing else he could do. This was not something you wanted to see. Not something that you could just throw away.

'Is she?'

'Yes,' said Perry. 'She's definitely dead. You don't survive that.'

He flopped against the wall, Susan still holding him. He was neither crying nor shaking. Instead, Perry was just silent.

Chapter 25

Macleod sat on the wooden bench he'd come to know by the side of Loch Ness. The view was quite something, but today he wasn't for views. He sat in his hat and coat, glad of them, for it was drizzling. Indeed, it might even have been rain by now, but Macleod was numb to it. He was waiting for Anna Hunt, and in truth, he wasn't sure he wanted to see her today. They had started out with such determination. He was going to bring people down, and they'd use that, they'd use the eagerness, the zest, to turn it around and pull the bluff.

Instead of having two warring factions, he did indeed now only have one. So, was there indeed a war anymore? The Forseti Group could disappear into the background and then operate when they wanted. The Revenge Group had been calling them out, the Revenge Group were showing where they were, and now with Bairstow dead, there was nothing. Indeed, the link into the McIntosh family was gone as well, with the death of the younger brother.

All the death, all the work, all the time spent on the Forseti Group and he was right back where they wanted him to be. He clenched his fist and then looked up to see a woman with

CHAPTER 25

black hair approaching. She wore a light rain jacket, but her head was uncovered and her hair was wet. She sat down, not opposite Macleod, but beside him.

'Are you okay?' she said. Macleod looked at her. 'I asked if you were okay. This isn't something you can talk to Hope about. So, I thought you might want to talk to somebody. I'm not in your team, so maybe that might make it easier as well.'

'Perry just saw someone blow their head off,' said Macleod.

'It's horrible,' said Anna. 'I've seen a couple of people not just do that, but do other similar things, and you never get immune to it.'

'We failed them as well. I wanted to arrest the Revenge group, but the Forsetis have just eliminated them, killed them, and they even did it within their ritual circle,' said Macleod.

'Exactly,' said Anna. 'What I can tell you is that your Chief Constable has resigned quietly. You'll find your friend Jim, the ACC, is going to step up into the role.'

'But what's the point?' said Macleod. 'We don't have anywhere to go. We're stuck. We blew it.'

'Clarissa's Frank's still alive. Clarissa's still alive. The rest of the team is still here. You shouldn't quit so easily.'

'What do you mean?' said Macleod.

'You shouldn't quit so obviously. The thing is, the Forseti group is now vulnerable.'

'How do you work that out?' asked Macleod.

'They've yanked the strings and everybody has danced to their tune. They must be feeling that they're on top of the world. The Revenge group is gone. They can do what they want. You have failed.'

Macleod hated the word, but it was true in this case.

'What they don't realise,' said Anna Hunt, 'is that this is your field for now. You haven't stopped.'

'Haven't I? What's the point now? We've got no leads. We've got nowhere to go. I am not putting my entire team in danger for a lost case.'

'Lost case? You are so up yourself sometimes. You're so melodramatic. Do you know that, Seoras?'

She reached over and put her hand on his, rubbing it. 'Do you know what my greatest quality is?'

'You mean something other than being able to put a bullet between a man's eyes at a hundred paces?'

'Sarky,' she said. 'This must have hurt you bad, because that's sarky for you.'

'Sorry,' he said.

'No, you're not. But understand this. My greatest quality is I don't stay down for good. I had an entire Service falling apart. People looking to kill me, looking to wipe us out. I'd lost all my trump cards. You haven't even got near that. And the Forseti group, well, they think they're safe. They think they're scot-free. That's when it becomes interesting.'

'How do you mean?' asked Macleod.

'You spend your time chasing people who know they've done something wrong. And they're looking over their shoulder, knowing that somebody's coming for them at some point. They may not know where you are. They may not know how you go about your business. But they sure as heck know somebody is coming at some point.

People feel at ease when they know somebody isn't. The Forseti group—you were coming after them. They humiliated you. Not in public. But they've humiliated you because you will beat yourself up since you failed to capture the top person. You failed in your duty as a police officer.'

CHAPTER 25

Macleod could feel her hand now, moving up his arm, round the back of his shoulder, and onto his neck. She started rubbing it without asking. He had to admit it was good. He had to admit something within him, albeit maybe the more animal side of him, was enjoying Anna Hunt's attention.

'You need to get at it, but you also need to learn that this is a silent war. You need to find him, but Seoras, you need to stay in the dark. Only when you're ready to go for the jugular, do you move.'

'I'm a detective chief inspector. I'm with the police. We don't work like that.'

'Some of you do. Think of it as gathering evidence.'

'What's the point of evidence? What's the point of evidence against somebody who can tamper with judges, can tamper with all the rest of it?'

'Because you know who it is,' said Anna. 'You know you've got the right person. So when you pull the trigger, you know it's okay.'

Macleod looked shocked beside her. 'That's not how I operate,' said Macleod.

Anna took her hand off his neck, turned and reached down into a bag she brought with her. She poured two coffees, and put one in front of Macleod. But the rain had come on heavier now, and he could see the splashes in the cup.

'We should probably get to cover,' said Macleod.

'We are not finished talking,' said Anna. 'You need to start again. You need to use your team carefully. Maybe this time, don't spread it so wide. Maybe this time use the person least likely. Back them up.'

'It strikes me that this is more of your sort of war,' said Macleod, 'something you could do, in the shadows, always in the shadows, no qualms about dispatching either.'

'Only because I satisfy myself that there's no other way to deal with them. This Forseti group is too dangerous. We need to capture them. We need to throw them in jail.'

'I would if I could,' said Macleod. He watched as Anna drank up her coffee. She then poured another one and drank it, then she tidied up, and finally she put everything in a bag. She turned back to Macleod. The rain was falling heavily now.

'I didn't want to say it out loud but nobody will hear a thing with this rain,' she said. 'Listen, I can't be sure that the Service still isn't compromised in different places, certain areas. So, you need to take up this fight. You need to keep it going. You need to turn around and tell the world at the end of it what happened.'

'But I can't continue a fight when there's no evidence. They shut the doors. Don't you get that?' said Macleod.

'You're right. They did shut the doors. They shut them all, or at least, they thought they had.' She then reached into her bag and put an envelope in front of Macleod. It had the simple inscription, 'Macleod.'

'What's this envelope?' he asked.

'It's not much,' said Anna, 'but it'll be enough to get going. Remember what I said. Engage the silent war. Not necessarily everybody. And also, whoever you use, we make sure they're in the right place.'

She went to turn away, but Macleod reached over and grabbed her arm. 'Thank you,' he said.

'I want this one,' she said. 'I really do. You may find, I might give a little more help now. Until next time.'

Macleod let her go, and then he opened up the envelope to find a piece of paper inside. When she was gone, Macleod

CHAPTER 25

stood up, the rain now teeming down. He walked over to the loch, looked at the water. He could see the little concentric circles that kept coming from the rain falling on it. But there was little wind, and the sea state must have been at least steady, if not slight at worst.

Silent war, he thought. And he looked at the loch and wondered about everything that was going on underneath. It was time to find this group, whatever the cost.

Read on to discover the Patrick Smythe series!

READ ON TO DISCOVER THE PATRICK SMYTHE SERIES!

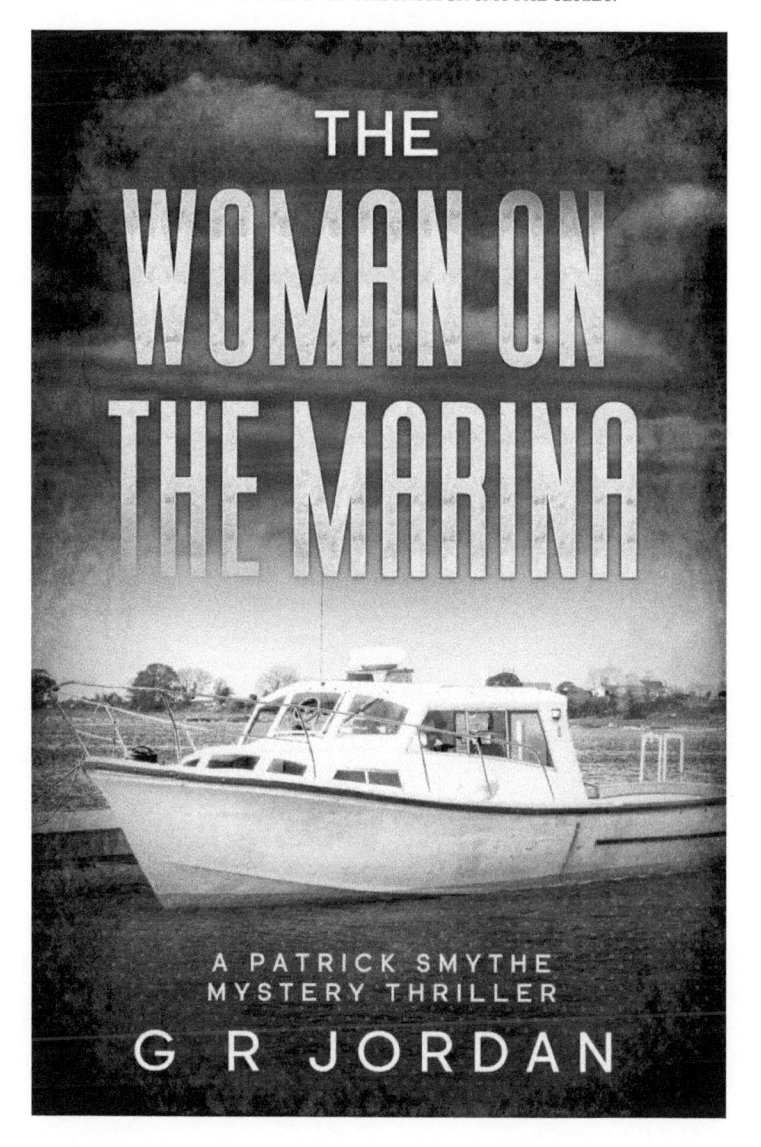

THE WOMAN ON THE MARINA

A PATRICK SMYTHE MYSTERY THRILLER

G R JORDAN

Patrick Smythe is a former Northern Irish policeman who after suffering an amputation after a bomb blast, takes to the sea between the west coast of Scotland and his homeland to ply his trade as a private investigator. Join Paddy as he tries to work to his own ethics while knowing how to bend the rules he once enforced. Working from his beloved motorboat 'Craigantlet', Paddy decides to rescue a drug mule in this short story from the pen of G R Jordan.

Join G R Jordan's monthly newsletter about forthcoming releases and special writings for his tribe of avid readers and then receive your free Patrick Smythe short story.

Go to https://bit.ly/PatrickSmythe for your Patrick Smythe journey to start

About the Author

GR Jordan is a self-published author who finally decided at forty that in order to have an enjoyable lifestyle, his creative beast within would have to be unleashed. His books mirror that conflict in life where acts of decency contend with self-promotion, goodness stares in horror at evil, and kindness blindsides us when we at our worst. Corrupting our world with his parade of wondrous and horrific characters, he highlights everyday tensions with fresh eyes whilst taking his methodical, intelligent mainstays on a roller-coaster ride of dilemmas, all the while suffering the banter of their provocative sidekicks.

A graduate of Loughborough University where he masqueraded as a chemical engineer but ultimately played American football, Gary had worked at changing the shape of cereal flakes and pulled a pallet truck for a living. Watching vegetables freeze at -40'C was another career highlight and he was also one of the Scottish Highlands "blind" air traffic controllers.

These days he has graduated to answering a telephone to people in trouble before telephoning other people to sort it out.

Having flirted with most places in the UK, he is now based in the Isle of Lewis in Scotland where his free time is spent between raising a young family with his wife, writing, figuring out how to work a loom and caring for a small flock of chickens. Luckily, his writing is influenced by his varied work and life experience as the chickens have not been the poetical inspiration he had hoped for!

You can connect with me on:
- https://grjordan.com
- https://facebook.com/carpetlessleprechaun

Subscribe to my newsletter:
- https://bit.ly/PatrickSmythe

Also by G R Jordan

G R Jordan writes across multiple genres including crime, dark and action adventure fantasy, feel good fantasy, mystery thriller and horror fantasy. Below is a selection of his work. Whilst all books are available across online stores, signed copies are available at his personal shop.

The Silent War (Highlands & Islands Detective Book 46

https://grjordan.com/product/the-silent-war

A police force in shock at a brutal act. The Forseti group target DCI Macleod's task force to save its skin. Can Macleod regroup his troops and allies and finish the war he was dragged into?

With the obliteration of the Revenge group, Macleod seeks to eradicate the Foresti group but finds himself on the defensive as the illicit society seeks to despatch Macleod from the scene. When tragedy strikes, Macleod finds his only path is an alliance with the Service and its less lawful methods. His honesty and integrity stretched, Macleod battles the greater good against his own conscience, wondering if he can end it all before more of his friends suffer. In a tense standoff, Macleod must chose between losing his very essence and bringing an end to the Forseti reign of terror.

Sometimes paying the price means you lose everything.

Kirsten Stewart Thrillers
https://grjordan.com/product/a-shot-at-democracy

Join Kirsten Stewart on a shadowy ride through the underbelly of the Highlands of Scotland where among the beauty and splendour of the majestic landscape lies corruption and intrigue to match any city. From murders to extortion, missing children to criminals operating above the law, the Highland former detective must learn a tougher edge to her work as she puts her own life on the line to protect those who cannot defend themselves.

Having left her beloved murder investigation team far behind, Kirsten has to battle personal tragedy and loss while adapting to a whole new way of executing her duties where your mistakes are your own. As Kirsten comes to terms with working with the new team, she often operates as the groups solo field agent, placing herself in danger and trouble to rescue those caught on the dark side of life. With action packed scenes and tense scenarios of murder and greed, the Kirsten Stewart thrillers will have you turning page after page to see your favourite Scottish lass home!

There's life after Macleod, but a whole new world of death!

Jac's Revenge (A Jac Moonshine Thriller #1)
https://grjordan.com/product/jacs-revenge

An unexpected hit makes Debbie a widow. The attention of her man's killer spawns a brutal yet classy alter ego. But how far can you play the game before it takes over your life?

All her life, Debbie Parlor lived in her man's shadow, knowing his work was never truly honest. She turned her head from news stories and rumours. But when he was disposed of for his smile to placate a rival crime lord, Jac Moonshine was born. And when Debbie is paid compensation for her loss like her car was written off, Jac decides that enough is enough.

Get on board with this tongue-in-cheek revenge thriller that will make you question how far you would go to avenge a loved one, and how much you would enjoy it!

A Giant Killing (Siobhan Duffy Mysteries #1)
https://grjordan.com/product/a-giant-killing

A body lies on the Giant's boot. Discord, as the master of secrets has been found. Can former spy Siobhan Duffy find the killer before they execute her former colleagues?

When retired operative Siobhan Duffy sees the killing of her former master in the paper, her unease sends her down a path of discovery and fear. Aided by her young housekeeper and scruff of a gardener, Siobhan begins a quest to discover the reason for her spy boss' death and unravels a can of worms today's masters would rather keep closed. But in a world of secrets, the difference between revenge and simple, if brutal, housekeeping becomes the hardest truth to know.

The past is a child who never leaves home!